EVE
Redemption

A Novel
By
Rebecca Tinkle

This is a work of fiction. Names, characters, places and incidents either are products of the author's imagination or are used fictitiously. Any resemblance to actual events or locales or persons, living or dead, is entirely coincidental.

Published by:
Love Today Organic Creations
Sedona, Arizona

dedication.

    I wrote this book for all of the women in the world who are working toward their own enlightenment. For any woman who ever fell in love with the wrong man or who followed her heart, only to realize that she made the wrong decision, suffered the consequences, but because of it became all the wiser. I wrote this book for every woman who is learning to love herself as she is, flaws and all.

    Writing this book was a sacred experience where I learned to embrace myself more with every page written. I found that as I let go of the judgments that I held about myself, I fell head-over-heels-in-love with the woman that I have become, realizing that I, like the character of Eve, was flawed but completely perfect. It is my hope that this book takes on the voice of whoever you may need: a best friend, confidant, mother, sister, teacher. It is my truest hope that this story brings you as deep of a gift as it brought me... the ability to love myself, in spite of myself, and the ability to trust myself above all others.

    This book is also for everyone who has supported me on this journey. *Especially the particular Tao Grand Master who woke me up, you know who you are...*

prologue.

My story is complicated. It has taken me eternities to live. I am sorry for everything that I've ever done. Every dark thing on this Earth exists because I could not erase the questions from my mind. Because I could not rest in the unspoken promise of the life that I was given. Because I dreamed of something more than paradise. Through my actions I unknowingly betrayed myself, every living being on this planet, and above all I have betrayed the very face of God.

For thousands of years I have heard from prophets *"The End is Near."* If only this were true, my arduous journey would soon be over. I have wished for this many times, yet if our story were to end now, our fate would not be the paradise that you think. That is why after all of this time I have come forward to share my story.

This is a story that has been told many times, in many different ways. You may think that you know the details, but you can't, for it has never been before told by the person who lived it: me.

I am Eve, mother of humanity.
This is my story.

Chapter 1
Present Day

Four church-bell chimes ring. I sit in the plush lobby of O.N.E. Earth executive offices, examining the room around me. Every extravagance has been extended to this architectural masterpiece. Each item is placed with an understated simplicity. Large windows frame a scenic view of New York City's Central Park. Through the window I watch life unfold as people walk, talk, jog, and busy themselves in the tasks of their lives. My fingers play with the corners of a mission statement that I have developed for the company's website. My eyes skim the introductory paragraph for the zillionth time.

"Founded by the world-renowned philanthropist Evan H. Stream; One Nation Enterprises: Earth, (O.N.E. Earth), manages a world-wide effort to assist the Earth and its inhabitants to create a more peaceful, productive world. Members of O.N.E. Earth diligently work toward the positive changes necessary to become more peaceable, tolerant and involved in the betterment of their communities. O.N.E. Earth is dedicated to peace, action, and human development. Our mission is to responsibly resolve the current economic, environmental, political and social challenges that this world faces. We believe in education and equality for all. All nations, all races, all creeds; we stand together as O.N.E."

"Anne." The receptionist calls my name, which is admittedly not the most effective way to elicit a response from me. I have had so many names over the years that it has become difficult to keep track of them all. I am partial to the name Anne, though. I was named after my current mother, who is by far my favorite of all of the women who have tended to my skinned knees and broken hearts. I had experienced hundreds upon hundreds of mothers over the years and have an intimate knowledge of the different variations motherhood can take. Each lifetime I get a new one, and having incarnated countless times, I am what you would call an expert daughter. Some have been good, some bad, some loved me without effort, while others tried, but fell into abusive patterns passed down by their own mothers. The family that I am born into is *the luck of the draw*, as the Gambler would say.

This multitude of feminine caretakers has given me an inside look at the hearts of the women on this planet, and an opportunity to experience the triumphs and foibles of life with them. It has been a way for me to stay connected, keep my finger on the pulse of humanity. I have watched the women around me progress over the years, evolve. This evolution of our sisterhood lead me to Beverly Anne, my current mother, the woman after whom I am named.

I am quite beautiful, as one would expect of the mother of humanity. My never-changing face has accompanied me throughout all of time. Sometimes my skin is as pale as the winter's moon, other times, a deep ebony. I have a face that looks natural with any ethnicity; though I will admit in some cultures my face has been considered awkward. Nose too small, eyes too round. But my uniqueness has always been considered a beautiful one, strange though it may have been.

I change bodies as one would change shoes. Some are comfortable and cozy, others painful and awkward. Heredity has given me bodies slim and long like a ballerina, others short and stout. In this lifetime I inherited my father's curls, more strawberry than blonde, pale skin, and freckles. I also inherited his annoying propensity to grow a little round belly. Yes, as cliché as it sounds, I, the mother of humanity, struggle to keep myself at a healthy weight. I've found it all but impossible to ingest carbs in this lifetime. I miss pasta. Better luck next time, I hope.

What made my mother of this lifetime so special was not her outward, but her inward beauty. Her face was lit from within. She used to tell me that the light of God was the best skin cream on the market. In quiet moments, her beauty shone through her face like the sun. And it was in the spaces between those moments that one could catch her essence, and her unspoken strength. What made her special was that she was *real*. She was comfortable in her own skin and confident in the woman she was. She was quiet, she was wise, she was beautiful, and she was, in her own way, enlightened.

My heart swells with the memory of her. I am proud to have called her mother. Because of her I found the reason to fight for a change: Love. And that is why I am here working for O.N.E. Earth, for my mother, who is also my great, great, great, great granddaughter and as all women, my direct descendant.

"Anne?" The receptionist clears her throat, raising an eyebrow. I hadn't noticed her addressing me until she appended the inflection of a question after my name.

"I'm sorry, lost in thought," I apologize with a smile. "I'm back."

"Mr. Stream will see you now." She returns the smile. I follow her down a circular hallway past rows of windowed executive offices and assistant desks. The entire floor is silent; I hear only the whisper of my footsteps as they move along the carpet. We come to a large stainless steel door. As she holds the door open for me to enter, a burst of sunlight floods the space around us. I love the feeling of the sun on my skin. My eyes take in the exterior wall of the executive office, which is comprised of floor to ceiling windows tinted in silver. The ceiling, painted the color of the summer sky, features individual crystal chandeliers with pinpoints of light that remind me of icicles. I pause to consider the message that the artist meant to convey through this obvious contradiction of warm and cold elements. To my left, a four foot blue statue of the Buddha is on display, folded hands rest on its lap, in the center of the palm a tear shaped diamond shimmers. The Buddha faces a large stainless steel desk. Behind the desk sits the founder of the Corporation. He smiles, standing to cross the distance as he offers his hand.

"Anne. It's nice to finally meet you." He envelopes my hand with both of his. His hands are warm, just like the streams of sunlight shining through the window. The experience of this room is cozy. I feel as if I am being welcomed home, though I have never been here before. Our eyes meet, his brow relaxes and he smiles. His nose is perfect, long and straight, thin bridge, pointed tip. I have never seen its equal; it is as if Michelangelo himself sculpted it. Airbrushed skin of bronze, not a single pore is visible on this perfect canvas. His face has a freshness that proclaims caviar facials and Evian baths. His cheeks flush with the glow of health. He looks more like a yacht-sailing model than a New York businessman. He doesn't rush to speak, he is not uncomfortable with silence. He allows a moment for us to simply be in each other's presence. Admittedly it is intoxicating, to feel the space where two souls meet for the first time without the distraction of words. This interaction reminds me of years passed, before the rush of industry, when times were truly simple. He smiles again with simple sincerity, and looks at me as if I'm his long lost best friend.

"Mr. Stream, the pleasure is mine," I say, breaking the silence.

"Call me Evan. Mr. Stream is what my mother calls me when she's feeling particularly cross toward me." He pauses to consider, "I'm certain that in time you will be tempted to call me that, as well. But for now, Evan will do."

He possesses an easy charm that delights, and an organic air that impresses me. He also has that money glow to him. The kind that you get when you have a lot, and always have. It's a radiance that proclaims to the world: I can have what I want, do what I want, and have had only the best in life. It's a glow that I myself have enjoyed many-a-lifetime, but not in this one. In this incarnation, loved though I may have been, my familial pattern has been one of oppression of expression and suppression of desire. This pattern of struggle was ingrained within me since birth, and being the dutiful daughter I have carried on the family legacy. It's every child's duty to carry the familial karma; that is, until you break the pattern. Which I haven't. I'm often exasperated and somewhat amused that I, the mother of humanity, live paycheck to paycheck. I blame Manolo Blahnik.

Evan is quite handsome. The proportions of his face harmonize with such perfection that I find it difficult to look away. Sky blue eyes dance with an exuberance for life, sun kissed skin, and golden spun hair with waves that catch the light. He stands with an easy dignity that commands the attention. And I am no exception. In fact, I'm distracted by the raw attraction that he emanates. Standing next to him I am suddenly *very* aware that I am a woman. His masculinity is so strong that every feminine instinct within me rises to balance the energy of the interaction. It's a natural, but unpracticed, instinct. I haven't met a man this powerful in eons. My mouth literally begins to water as my body naturally prepares itself to kiss this man.

I'm horrified at my barbaric instinct to club this man and drag him to my cave. I remind myself that this compulsion isn't appropriate in this setting. *He is my boss. I must remain professional.* I clear my throat, looking for a moment to regain an air of asexual professionalism. *Focus on something else, anything else.* I turn to the statue of the Buddha.

"This is quite unusual." *Small talk is good.* I inhale and count to three. "I don't recognize the stone. What is it?" I take another deep breath to gather these rampant senses. *I can't believe this man's mere presence has such a powerful effect on me.* I haven't felt this type of attraction since long ago. Too many lifetimes to count. Evan smiles as if he can see the battle going on within me. It's obvious that women respond to him in this way often, and he finds it amusing. He steps behind me, inches away. I lean closer to the statue in a lame attempt to create distance between us. My breath is short, skin hot. The intensity of my body's response to his physicality unnerves me. I hate not having control over myself. I've spent lifetimes in meditation to acquire the ability to harness my desires and with one fell swoop this man has broken down my barriers. Desire overtakes will. My blood boils with equal parts infuriation and arousal. I know it isn't rational, but I am mad at him.

"It's my prize piece," he explains. "The Buddha is carved from Azurite, which is said to possess the power to transform fear into understanding. And this," he leans past me, brushing my arm with his as he motions to the stone cupped in the Buddha's hand, "This is the Millennium Star diamond." The closer he draws near, the further I lean away from him. He *has* to be doing this on purpose; either that or he has no concept of personal space. If I were to lean any closer to this statue, I would soon be kissing the Buddha on the lips. I feign interest in the diamond.

"This statue provides me inspiration when I forget what I'm working for," he pauses. When I turn, I find that he has taken a step back, eyes gleaming with some unseen vision. "Looking at this reminds me who I want to be. A leader, like the Buddha, made of the very substance that transforms fear into freedom. I, too, wish to hold humanity in my hands, beings that have the ability to shine - if, cut and polished in the proper way. And as you know, diamonds rarely polish themselves." He smiles, casting his eyes downward in a show of humility. "I know that might sound idealistic and exoteric, but it helps on the bad days when I forget what I am working for."

"That is the most beautiful thing I have heard in a long time." I am stunned. From his lips my own thoughts are dictated to me. "I haven't heard such pure idealism in years," I confess. In many ways Evan reminds me of the very man that he admires. He yearns just as the Buddha did, just as I do, for a better world. I knew Siddhartha before he became the *Buddha,* when he was still a *seeker* and not, for lack of a better word, a *finder.* I've never met anyone so sad. All the pain of the world weighed on his heart and was amplified by his desire for the world to be good. *All life is suffering,* he had said. He was depressed. He was indignant. He was desperate to be released from the wheel of karma, and to liberate the world from the same. The suffering on this Earth was a shock to his system, one from which he did not recover until his moment of illumination.

Siddhartha had been born into luxury. A prince who was destined to become a king that would one day conquer the world. Either that or he would become an impoverished spiritual leader who would attain enlightenment. That was the prophecy. For the great ones it can go either way. There is always a choice. You can choose great power, or surrender to God. He chose correctly, and now he has ascended. I envy him. I wish I had made the decision that he had, but as everyone knows, I chose power instead.

The first time he laid his eyes upon me after his enlightenment I saw them spark with recognition, and knew that he could see my deepest secrets. He saw past who I pretended to be into what I am. The mother of humanity. He saw my suffering and consoled me as I grieved for my own lack of illumination. What a relief it was to be able to share with another being the truth of my quest. In him, I found a confidant and a dear friend.

Evan reminds me of the many great masters that I have shared my lives with. He is one of the unlucky few, who like Atlas, supports the weight of the world on their shoulders. Perhaps this unnerving attraction toward Evan is simply an indication of the many great things that we can achieve together. Perhaps I misinterpreted the message of my body's response. It wasn't a sexual compulsion that my body was trying to express, but a more noble desire for partnership. Perhaps the heat in my body wasn't indicating an attraction to him as a man, but the possibilities that our efforts could produce together for the world.

With the Buddha, and every ascended master I have met since, I have shared a comradery. It wasn't necessary for me to lie about my identity. Together we contemplated, practiced the same regimes, and willed our souls to return to the Creator. But something unseen has kept me tethered to this plane. No master has ever held an answer for me. I have been fated to be born time and again, lifetime after lifetime, with full knowledge of all my previous lifetimes, to directly experience the world I have created, until the end. For me, there have been no short cuts. *Maybe Evan was the key. Maybe this time would be different.* Maybe my body was sending me a message to wake up and pay attention.

Adam never understood my yearning for absolution. He never possessed the same fire that I have inside. I can't blame him, he could never know what it's like to be the catalyst for the fall of man. Every dark thing on this Earth, every ugly intention, every harsh circumstance weighs on my heart as if it were my own. Even still, late at night when all are asleep, my soul calls to the heavens for redemption. Sometimes my longing is so intense that it expresses itself as rage, sometimes as tears, but always with hope. That is, also, why I am here, working for O.N.E. Earth.

Evan places his hand on my arm. "Are you ready?"

"To transform humanity?"

He laughs, the amusement of an unexpected joke dances in his eyes. "Anne, you little dear. I can see that we're going to be fast friends." He reaches his hand to clasp my shoulder in a long arm embrace. "Actually, I was referring to the updated mission statement." He squeezes my shoulder and smirks.

"Oh Evan, I'm sorry." I can't believe how off-kilter I feel. His warm palm on my shoulder disorients me, the heat in my body rises another degree. I'm hardly able to take my attention off of him long enough to ground myself. Shaking my head, I try to reset my thoughts. "I'm ready."

"Come." He takes my arm to lead me to the chair opposite his at the desk.

"This is just a draft, I welcome suggestions," I explain, as I pass the document across the table. He slips on a pair of black framed glasses and begins to read. I examine his handsome face to measure his response, though his expression reveals nothing. When he is finished he sits back and gazes out the window, deep in thought. I shift my eyes to the table, allowing him a moment to meditate on what he has just read.

"It needs work," he says, furrowing his brow. "It needs to be more relevant to the average person. Everyone *says* that they want to live a better life, have a better community, a better world, but when it comes down to taking action in the midst of daily life, well, there is just no motivation. Your work here," -- he motions to the document -- "reflects the *let's-hold-hands-and-have-peace* aspect, which is good. But we have to come up with a concept that will engage the reader into immediate, measurable action. I don't want this to just be words on a paper, *I want it to be alive*." He glances at his watch, "Do you have plans for dinner? We can get this hammered out in a couple of hours."

"For world peace? I can stay a couple more hours," I say, feeling my heart double beat at the thought of sharing a meal with him.

"There's a quiet restaurant down the street where we can grab a bite and get some work done," he says, handing me the portfolio as he stands. He turns on one heel and glides across the four feet of space behind his desk to the silver steel wall. A push of two fingers reveals a hidden compartment, where he retrieves a gray wool overcoat. He looks back, our eyes lock in a glance that causes a burst of adrenaline in my belly, and if I was honest, a little below as well. "Do we need to stop by your office and grab your jacket?"

"I drove into the city today." I shake my head, "I didn't expect to leave the building."

"You can borrow one of mine," he says. Instead of slipping the jacket over his own shoulders, he holds it open for me.

"Thank you," I say, craning my neck as I feed my arms into its too long sleeves. I'm hyper aware that my body is now wrapped in wool that has caressed his skin, and it thrills me. My fingers move to fasten the buttons along the front of the jacket, but something causes me to pause. I take a deep breath in and my senses reel. My mind dashes wildly in all directions as it tries to recall a vague sense memory long forgotten. *I know this scent from somewhere.* It's both familiar and intoxicating - musky, masculine, with just a hint of magnolia. I have to restrain myself from rubbing my face into the cloth of his coat, behaving like a feline with a new catnip toy. *What's the matter with me today?* My eyes flit inadvertently to his jaw, the source of this scent, and my feminine instincts urge me to run my lips along its surface. My ears feel hot, which means that a blush has bloomed on my cheeks. *I must get hold of myself.* Taking a deep breath, I try to put my attention in my lower abdomen, a technique that I learned from a Tao master to ground myself, though I know that this will do little good. I'm already too enthralled. I can hardly breathe.

"Ready?" Evan places his hand in the small of my back.

"Ready," I exhale. I take long, conscious breath to calm the butterflies dancing in my stomach. *I have a feeling that this is going to be a very interesting night.*

Chapter 2

We settle into the private dining room at Picholine on West 64th street. Its wooden walls lined in fine wines, dimmed lights, and white table settings lull me into a state of comfortable luxury. The perfect combination of aged wood, wine and a subtle array of spices flood my senses.

"Would you like a glass of wine?" Evan asks, resting his gaze on me as he leans forward attentively.

"Please," I whisper, inclining my head. This is starting to feel more like a date than a business meeting.

Evan summons the server who stands in wait at the edge of the room. "We'll take a bottle of the Jaboulet, La chapelle 1990, thank you." He hands the wine list to the server.

"A fine choice Mr. Stream, sir."

"Evan, please." Evan dismisses the formality.

"Yes, of course, Mr. Stream." The server bows and turns to exit.

Evan turns to me and shakes his head. "You know Anne, after you have acquired a certain amount of wealth; no one remembers your first name. It's as if the money causes amnesia."

"So... *Evan.* I'm curious what has brought you here, to this?" I motion toward the space he occupies, "What in your life has led you to this ardent mission to save the world?"

He leans back in his chair. Gray cashmere rustles over a well-defined chest and a thousand storms of yesteryear crash behind his eyes. His stormy expression causes me to lean forward in my chair, anticipating a great revelation.

"Deplorable beginnings," he says.

I narrow my eyes, "That can't be it?"

"I had a rocky beginning," he explained. "The first part of my life was spent in the selfish pursuit of power. I stepped on a lot of people and made a mess of my life. I realized the extent of the damage that I had caused, both to myself, and others, and knew that I needed to change. That is why I am here, on a quest for redemption." The corner of his lip pulls in a sad smile, "And what is your story? What has led you to me, trying to save the world?"

I cast my eyes to the table, shaking my head. "It's complicated," I confess, my voice just above a whisper.

"I'm interested," he says, leaning forward.

"I guess I've been trying to save the world, in my own way, for a long time. But I am but one woman, and the problems of the world are complex and numerous. I used to think that it didn't matter, that one voice could reach the multitudes… but the longer that I live, the less that seems likely. I had all but given up, resigning myself to the predetermined fate of humanity. Then, I found you."

"You found me?" he asks, raising an eyebrow.

"I saw you giving a lecture on television. As you spoke I felt something in my heart that I hadn't felt in a long time."

"What was that?" he asks.

"Something in what you said, perhaps the way that you said it, gave me hope. I couldn't resist being a part of it."

"That's the answer that you would give your boss, Anne. I want the real answer. I want to know why your heart blazes for a better world." He lifts his wine glass, swirling the contents.

"What makes you think that my heart blazes?" I ask.

He places the wineglass on the table, "I've heard how hard you work, the hours you put in. Your passion is infamous. That's why I wanted to meet you. I was curious to meet the girl that works harder than me." He picks up the glass and takes a sip. "Why does your heart blaze, Anne?" he asks, again.

"It's not one thing in particular, Evan." I smile as I speak, though I can feel the sadness seep from my eyes. "I'm just heartbroken at the condition of the world. Sometimes I feel so depressed with my life, with this place, that it's hard to find the motivation to get out of bed. It seems pointless at times. I've been in some dark places. It's far worse than ever and I just want it all to end."

"As in, you want the world to end? Then you are in the wrong company. I intend to keep it here for a long time," he says, raising an eyebrow.

"I don't want the world to end, just the game." I stop short. *Did I just say that?*

"What game, Anne?" Evan leans forward. I have caught his attention.

Chiding myself for not being more careful; I resolve to not allow the slightest hint of my past to emerge. I'm too comfortable around him, and that is dangerous. I backtrack, "I just see the world as one big game for power. Those who have it suffer to maintain it, those who don't have it suffer to get it, or give up hope because they don't think that they ever will. I just want the power struggles to end so that we can live as equals."

"Usually someone who works so hard to redeem something feels as if they need redemption, too. What are trying to redeem, Anne?" Evan watches me as he leans back.

"Deplorable beginnings," I say, mirroring his earlier response.

"It looks like we have a lot in common."

"Indeed."

He furrows his brow, deep in thought. "Ocean or mountains?"

"What?"

"Which do you prefer?"

"Okay, that's random." I laugh.

"Humor me." Between his index fingers he pivots the candle.

"Alright. Ocean," I concede. What could be the harm in a little get-to-know-you game?

A wicked smile passes his lips, "Chocolate or Vanilla?"

I laugh. "Both."

"You can't choose both."

"Alright, *white* chocolate."

"That's cheating," he chastises. "Day or night?"

"Night."

"I figured."

"Really. How?"

"You remind me of moon-flowers. It's a night bloom, hence the name." He extends his arm across the table to run his index finger along the back of my hand, the slow intimacy of which both relaxes and excites me. "See…? Your skin, it's so delicate and pale. And softer than it looks."

I shift my hand back to neutral territory and change the subject. "Your turn… sunrise or sunset?"

He laughs as if I have just told a joke. I raise my eyes to meet his,

"What's funny about that?" I ask, amused.

"Nothing," he replies, stifling his laughter. "Sunset, definitely. The best things in my life always happen at sunset."

Curiosity cocks my head, "Like what?"

"I fell in love at sunset. But that was many years ago."

"Who is this mystery woman? Will I meet her?" I ask, carefully concealing my disappointment at this recent revelation.

He leans forward, the air shifts between us. "She is lost," he explains, a sad smile pulling at the corner of his lip again.

"Lost?" my voice softens. "What happened? Nothing terminal, I hope."

"I meant that she is lost to me. I betrayed her."

"That doesn't sound like something that you would do."

"Deplorable beginnings, remember?"

"I'm sure that you could talk to her, apologize," I offer.

Evan leans back and looks toward the ceiling as if to offer a silent prayer. "Once you have broken the heart of a woman who loved you without question; that is a hard one to overcome. Hell hath no fury, or so they say."

This time it is my hand that reaches across the table. I cover his with mine; the warmth between us melts any trouble in my mind. With one touch the heaviness of my past fades to nothingness. I let my hand linger. The image of our bodies twisted in crisp, white sheets weaves through my imagination; it is so thrilling that I can hardly return to the reality of this restaurant, but when I do, Evan's eyes are on mine. "You can't live your life according to archaic platitudes. Talk to her. I'm sure she would understand."

He turns his hand over and cradles my palm in his. He contemplates my flesh as he traces the contours of my hand. I wonder how I could have spent an eternity *not* feeling his touch. It is as natural and a part of me as every breath I take.

"Perhaps," his tone dismisses the feasibility of my suggestion. "Can I ask you a question, Anne?"

"Of course," I concede.

"What does your Utopia look like?"

When I breathe, the breath fills me. As if after years of taking air without nourishment, the breath of life has been granted me once more. I'm too old to believe in love at first sight. I'm almost too old to believe in love at all, not here on Earth, but something about this man lets me *almost* believe.

"You mean heaven on earth? That's a big question, Evan."

"I'm sure that you have a big answer," his voice is laden with sincerity. "You strike me as someone who would know."

"Haven't you been listening?" I laugh. "I told you. I can be quite the depressive. Why would you assume that I know what heaven is like?"

"I suspect that your depression comes from living in a world that doesn't live up to your standards. It's natural that you have been depressed. I have a theory that the ones that suffer the most from depression here;" – he motions round about him -- "are the closest to heaven, *here*." He reaches over the table to touch the center of my chest with such compassion that my eyes burn with lifetimes of unshed tears. I'm moments away from a tearful confession of my life's greatest laments when I remember who I am and why I am here. *Evan is my boss, and this is a business meeting.* I pull my hand back abruptly and straighten my spine,

"Evan, maybe we should focus?"

"As you wish," he concedes. "So, what does your Utopia look like?" he asks again.

"Evan?" the tone of my voice borders on pleading. "Let's just stick to business, please?"

He holds his hands up. "This *is* business. Have you forgotten the industry we work in?"

"You win, on a technicality." I exhale, "Utopia can be a hard one to define. To boil it down, it is life without all of the mental and social systems." I sum up my opinion in one technical sentence, explaining only the mechanics of it. I can't go there, describing what I know from experience to be paradise on Earth. I resolved long ago not to return to Paradise in daydream only. It only makes it harder, and things are difficult enough.

"Well that's not the answer that I expected," he laughs. "I mean, that's a plain faced way of putting it. I imagined that you would have painted me a lyrical picture filled with lavish descriptions and adjectives." He shakes his head, smiling, "You *are* a paradox. I will accept that answer, for now," he promises.

"Maybe forever," I breathe, implying that my lips will remain sealed. "Your turn. How do you see Utopia?"

"Life without all of the mental and social systems," he teases.

"Cheater." I allow myself to relax. I'm tired of reminding myself to remain professional. "Do you think that we can really do it… affect a change on the Earth?"

"Part of me thinks, yes, the other thinks, no. But a man has to work toward a noble goal. Shoot for the moon and you may reach the stars."

"And *that* is not the answer that I expected from you."

"Looks like I may be a paradox as well, yes?"

"Perhaps we both have lived too long and seen too much," I offer. "And are stupid enough to hope for more, or smart enough. I'm not sure which."

"Then we make a good pair," he states decidedly.

"So it seems." And it did. Against all odds, I'd finally found someone as idealistic and complex as me. I wonder how such a young man could have developed such depth. He couldn't be more than thirty. People would describe him as an old soul, which I know is a fallacy. There are no such beings, other than me and Adam, *and we are more than old, we are ancient.*

"Anne."

"Yes?"

"Are you married?"

"Recently divorced," I answer, just above a whisper.

"Oh, right… I heard. I'm sorry."

"Thank you," I answer shortly, hoping he doesn't pry. I couldn't go into the details of my first love, my eternal life-long partner, Adam, leaving me. I couldn't explain that after thousands of lifetimes together he became too depressed to look into my eyes, for there he saw a constant reminder of all we had lost. I couldn't explain that the cherished face that had greeted me into this world so long ago had turned from me, vowing never to return.

We were a lot like teenagers in the beginning, Adam and I. We discovered the world and each other in the slowest, sweetest love story of all time. It was a time when holding hands could thrill me beyond measure and we could find the world in each other's eyes. It was epic. It was endearing. It was innocent. And it was doomed. It's ironic that it was Adam who left our relationship. He had never wavered in his faithfulness to me and his love endured long after it should have. I was always more complicated than he was. I could never tell if that complication was what kept his interest peaked all those lifetimes, or if it was something he endured because he loved the girl under all the turmoil. His troubles began the moment my eyes opened for the first time. But he couldn't see that. He was too blinded by love. But in the end, it was too much for him. *I* was too much for him. He had no choice, but to leave me.

For the first time in my long life, I am truly alone.

"What happened?"

"It's complicated."

"It usually is."

We sip our wine in silence.

"Ready to get to work?" he asks, graciously changing the subject.

"Yes," I say, relieved.

"Eve."

"Yes?"

Wait. What? My eyes narrow. "What did you just call me?"

"Eve," Evan repeats the name, his eyes search my face.

Could it be?

No. Impossible.

After all this time he had returned to claim me as his own?

Chapter 3
The Beginning

The first breath was the best. Of all of the lifetimes, of all of the first breaths that I have taken, that one was the best. How that sweet breath was breathed into me, filling my lungs, traveling like a cool fire throughout my entire body. Then I felt a pulse, surging through me. As I breathe in and out I feel my awareness expanding to my face, brightening in relaxed waves of light. A circular expansive energy travels through the back of my head, down my spine, through my legs and feet; circulating up my shins, abdomen, and chest, feathering through the planes of my face once more in soft waves of life. I didn't breathe my first breath; it was breathed into me.

I was.
I am.
Life.

****

I stretch my body. The deeper I stretch, the more intense the pleasure, the movement activating the muscles in my feet and legs. It all feels breathtakingly good, like my body is supposed to move this way. With a moan of pleasure I stretch my arms, opening my eyes only when my fingertips brush against something soft and warm; it feels like liquid gold, amber and rich.

I turn my head to discover the cause of this sensation on my fingertips. A man with shining eyes stares at me tenderly, a hint of moisture glimmering in their corners. I recognize him. He is me, as I am him. We are one and the same, yet occupy separate spaces.

"Hi." He cocks his head, raising a hand to pull his fingers through a short crop of brown curls. "I'm Adam," he taps his chest, speaking slowly enough for me to comprehend. His face is a perfect symmetry of strong lines. Straight thin nose that slopes downward to a long point, strong jaw, full pale pink lips upturned at the corners, flawless skin, soft and pure. He holds his hand out for mine. As I place my hand in his, a magical energy plays between our palms. The texture of our flesh fascinates me, I can feel every ridge in our hands slide with intimate friction as he pulls me upright, to his eye level. Awe shines from his auburn eyes as he cradles my face in his palms; his thumbs tracing the peaks of my cheekbones. The silence is pregnant with hopeful expectation. He draws my head down to kiss my forehead, the warmth from his lips radiates a golden starburst of love that weaves through my flesh. An unfamiliar instinct urges me to drop my head onto his chest. Each beat of his heart lulls me into a comfortable relaxation as I nestle into him. I feel so safe, so warm, content and natural. After a long moment he speaks,

"You're perfect," he whispers.

I look up at his face to orient myself. "Perfect?" I ask. "Is that my name?"

He looks surprised. "You understand me?"

"Yes."

His smile blooms, "You can talk?"

"Yes," I smile.

He laughs, hugging me. "You *are* perfect!" He kisses the top of my head.

"Is that what I should be called? Perfect?" I test the word on my lips.

He laughs again, this time the sound of it fills the air around us, "There is a name that is even more perfect than Perfect." He looks into the distance and deliberates, "Look."

My gaze follows his. The sun dips behind the horizon; warm, rich colors play inside of the clouds. "I have never seen anything more beautiful than the setting sun. That is, until I gazed upon *your* face." He runs a finger down the bridge of my nose, "You shall be called *Eve*, in honor of the moment that I first discovered your face welcoming the moon into the sky."

"What is the moon?"

"It's what lights the night and gives life to the stars. You'll see. It's almost time." He pulls me to his side, lying in the grass. Resting my head in the crook of his arm, a delicious tiredness settles over me. Relaxation drifts through my body in waves as Adam and I watch the sun descend past the horizon, and the moon casts her spell across the night sky. The peace of the night overtakes me, and Adam and I explore each other with our fingertips, tracing the contours of each other's bodies until sleep claims us both.

****

At dawn, I am awakened by three drops of the sweetest nectar dripping onto my lips. The flavor bursts on my tongue with intensity. My eyes fly open. Adam is above me, looking down with the most ridiculous smile. He holds the dripping sacrament in his hand.

"*What* is that?"

"This is called an orange," he smiles. "Amazing, right?"

I nod, eyes wide. "May I have more?"

"As much as you'd like. There are thousands more just like it." He pulls me to my feet and tows me behind him, the muscles in my legs burn with exertion. "See, there are trees everywhere!" he shouts, lifting me in his arms to spin me through the air. His gorgeous skin flushes with excitement.

I look around to see the multitude of trees holding the same round orange spheres in their long arms.

He continues, speaking almost too quickly for me to comprehend, "This is called food. There are many different types to choose from. See?" He sets me down to pluck another round sphere in the shade of red from a nearby tree and bites into it. "Mmmmmm," he exhibits how delicious the fruit is by closing his eyes and chomping in abandon with such enthusiasm that I have to laugh. One eye peeks open to measure my response as he offers me the fruit that he has just bitten into. "This is called an apple."

I hold the fruit in my hand and test the word, "Apple."

I sink my teeth into its flesh. The crisp fruit makes a loud krrrrck as I bite into it; its juice travels down my chin. It's sweet like the orange, but in a different way. It's both juicy and dry at the same time. I take another bite, closing my eyes as I am immersed in the rush of flavors that burst on my tongue. I can taste the Earth, the sun, and the air, intermingling with the sweetest hint of life. Adam snatches the apple from my hand and pitches it over his shoulder.

"Hey!" I complain.

Adam laughs, grabbing my hand, "This is *just* the beginning!" He takes me from tree to tree to sample all of the different fruits that are ours for the taking. Peaches, pears, plums, figs, grapes, lemons, cherries; each holds a delightful surprise. After we have sampled the array of fruits, we sit under a peach tree. Adam is perched above me on a low hanging branch, licking the last of the juice from his fingers.

"Are all of them round?"

"All of what?"

"The fruits. Are they always round?"

He smiles, mischief glints in his eyes, "Not all of them. There is one that is, different." He jumps down and offers his hand, "I'll show you."

Pulling me behind him, he leads me deep into the orchard where we find a clearing in the center of the garden. Without a word, our eyes take in the glory of the scene before us. The clearing is a perfect circle with two majestic trees located in the center. I step forward. As my foot crosses the threshold my body is engulfed in a rising heat; at the same time clear cold air rushes down my body. As the two sensations meet I'm filled with an inexplicable glee. Fascinated, I step closer to examine these two mystical trees.

The first tree is tall and narrow with high branches. The leaves are many; small silver green wings that blow gently in the breeze. The tree bears fruit in the shape of a cube, which is transparent and filled with a liquid white light that glows through the casing. The breeze that blows through the leaves tickles the fruit and the tree seems to tinkle with a quiet laughter. The entire tree is aglow with a silver white light.

The second tree, ten feet away, is much shorter and plush. Its far-reaching branches expand majestically from a solid white trunk. An intricate play of golden embroidery weaves its way through the trunk, shifting and moving through the bark, creating and recreating the most beautiful scenes. Birds, lion, man, vast skies and cumulous clouds. It is as if the tree tells the very tale of creation. Its fruit, warm amber spheres that shine like hundreds of miniature suns. The colors in the molten fruit shift constantly and hum audibly with life.

Mesmerized, I walk toward the trees, "I thought you said there was only one tree? I see two."

Behind me, Adam responds, "You asked if there was a tree that had fruit that was *not* in the shape of a sphere, I said there was one, *and this is it*." A wry smile passes his lips as he motions toward the first tree with its incandescent cubes of light.

The moment my eyes alight upon the tree of stars, with its twinkling cubes of light, I am overcome by surges of power radiating from the *other* tree, the sun-lit tree directly in front of me. It radiates such power that it demands my attention, almost as if it were jealously calling me back. When my attention returns, I am rewarded. My soul fills with a pulsing warmth, shifting every cell in my body in a kaleidoscopical dance. Continuous shifts of energy take my breath away. If the tree makes me feel like this just by looking at it, I can't imagine how it would feel to *taste* it.

"What is *this* one called?" I breathe, with much effort, as my body vibrates in a subtle cosmic dance, each moment individuated and separate from the last. In a slow shutter of images, my hand rises to touch one of the amber spheres with my fingertips. The temperature of the air becomes dramatically warmer as my hand draws near.

"Eve! Don't!" Adam exclaims.

Startled, I turn, "What? Why?"

Adams becomes serious, "It is The Tree of the Life. Its nectar is too powerful for us; we would die if we ate of it."

I look back toward the tree in wonder. I can see his point. I don't know if I could live through the pleasure of tasting this fruit when just looking at it leaves me breathless. "It's so beautiful," I whisper as I brush the surrounding air with my fingertips, careful not to make direct contact; my hand overflows with a sensation of life.

Adam pulls me into an intimate embrace. Our bodies melt into each other, fused by the powerful tree. I can't tell where I end and he begins. I turn my attention toward the first tree, the tree of stars. Without thinking, my fingers rise toward its silvery fruit of light.

"And this one?" I pull my hand back, a chill touches my bone. Adam takes my hand and warms it between his palms.

"That is called the Tree of the Knowledge of Good and Evil. It's fruit is called Pandora."

I contemplate this information, "And this one would kill us too?"

Adam looks deep into my eyes. "Eve, what happened to your hand when it neared it?"

I look at my palm between Adam's. "It was cold. It hurt…" I answer, moving my fingers to restore circulation.

"Well, then you wouldn't want to eat it, would you?"

"No, of course not," I agree, shaking my head.

Adam takes my hand and leads me to the place from where we came. "You should have *seen* the look on your face when you saw the trees," he says, reenacting my expression of shock and awe when my eyes first took in the trees of light. He's adorable, there is no question. I'm thankful that he is my guide in this garden.

"They are beautiful," I agree, looking back toward the trees, one brilliant as the moon, its fruit twinkles like the stars. The other, majestic as the sun, radiating warmth and power. "Would it be okay to come back again?"

"Everything here is for us to enjoy, the trees being no exception. Just remember; no eating them." He spins around abruptly, surprising me, "Because they are poisonous!" he growls and leaps. We tumble to the ground.

"Adam!" I laugh as he devours me with snarling teeth and scratching paws.

"Shhh… I'm eating," he growls, attempting to coax me into compliance by biting my shoulder.

"Ouch, Adam! Stop!" I laugh, attempting to crawl away. He catches my waist and flips me onto my back, settling himself over my body to rest his weight on his elbows. Each part of our bodies lay in contact, skin to skin, from toes to nose. Adam licks the tip of my nose and plants one beautiful kiss upon my lips,

"Remember how dangerous they are, okay?"

"I understand," I reply, smiling at my companion. He is everything good, and I love him. I'm so happy to be alive. I feel like the whole world, and everything in it, was made just for us.

****

Something inside of me has shifted since meeting the trees of light located in the clearing. Every time that I think of them - an equally exciting and uncomfortable sensation rumbles through my blood. Before, I was free to enjoy the subtle gift that every moment brought, moving from one moment to the next without a thought of the past or hope for what the future moment may bring. But now, my thoughts jump between the memory of the trees and the dream of what it will feel like the next time that I am in their presence. These leaps of mind through time and space have created a feeling of anxiousness within my body – an emptiness that begs to be filled. And yet, I cannot control my mind.

I want to be near them. I want to listen to the varying tinkles and hums that each makes. They produce a kind of music, both heard by the ear and felt by the heart. I want to lay at their roots, climb their branches, and bathe in their glow. The more I want, the worse I feel. Even still, the act of longing is somehow intoxicating. Adam notices my mood and inquires,

"Eve? Where are you? You've hardly said a word all night."

"Hmmm?" I mumble, pulled from thought.

Adam responds as if my response were humorous; "I asked what you were thinking?" He sinks to sit near my feet. Absentmindedly, I twist his curls around my fingers,

"Those trees you took me to see today… I can't figure out why they would be forbidden to us. I mean, there has to be a reason, right?"

Adam runs his fingers along my calf. "Well, I suppose that they are too powerful. Maybe our bodies couldn't handle the nectar."

"But if the fruit is too powerful, then why put it in the garden in the first place? For us *not* to eat? Why not make our bodies strong enough to ingest it? It just doesn't make sense."

"There must be a good reason, and I'm sure we'll find out. For now, we'll just have to trust that the Creator has his reasons." Adam's easy answer annoys me.

My lazy caress moves to his forehead, the pads of my fingers trace his face. He sighs, tilting his head to rest on my knee. "There is such a magic to them," I continue. "And the way they practically sing, it's the most beautiful thing that I have ever heard. The birds are put to shame in the presence of *that* song. I want to return in the morning. Do you want to come with me?"

My question is met with silence. I shift in my seat, feeling uneasy, as if perhaps my interest in the trees were somehow wrong. I backtrack, "I mean, if you think it would be okay. I won't touch them. I just want to listen to them, and look."

Again, no response.

"Adam?" My heart skips a beat, afraid that I have offended him somehow. I peek over his head to measure his response and find that he is fast asleep; a relaxed smile touches his lips. Relief washes through me. I scratch his head and muss his hair, the movement wakes him. He looks up and smiles, the remnants of a dream lingers in his eyes. He yawns once and drops his head to nuzzle my leg. I pull a fistful of his hair. My heart swells.

"Adam, I love you."

"I love you, too."

"Let's go to bed." Standing, I offer my hand to help him up. Taking my palm, he uses the resistance to pull himself to his feet, stretching his arms and arching his back. He moans, catching my shoulders with outstretched arms to pull me close. He kisses my forehead and rests his head against mine, holding me in his sleepy embrace.

"Do you want to come with me tomorrow?" I ask, grateful that he didn't hear my previous show of awkward backtracking.

"Hmmm? Where?" he yawns, again.

"To the clearing." I reply simply.

"Sure."

I hop up and down, excited, "Really?" I kiss his face, once, twice, three times. "Oh Adam, thank you!" I hug him, my affections awakened by sheer excitement. Surprised by my enthusiasm he bellows,

"We can go there every day!" He puffs his chest in a display of manliness, eyes dancing with the expectation of another kiss for his generous offer. I laugh at his ridiculous charm and kiss him again, and again, and again.

"And for tomorrow, and the next day, and the next day, and the next…" I sing between each kiss. He dips me back and nibbles my neck, growling like an animal about to devour. "Stop!" I twist out of his embrace and run.

Overtaken by primal instincts, he chases me. I scream as I fall into our bed of velvet leaves, Adam jumps on top, pins my arms above my head, and continues to nibble. He bites me, almost too hard, but I like it. I squirm to break the embrace. Squeals of laughter fill the room, and quite unexpectedly our gazes lock in an intent stare. I examine his bright brown eyes, there is so much joy and life behind them. I raise my fingers to caress his brow. Not a word is spoken, but everything is conveyed in that touch. It was a touch of sincere gratitude for the companionship that he offers. He is perfect, and joyful, and playful and mine. He pulls me closer, so close that our noses touch. His breath becomes steady and slow. I close my eyes and think about the joys that tomorrow will bring. I will see the trees again and get to take a much closer look at these two wondrous plants. It doesn't seem accurate to call them plants, for they are much more than that. The last image that floats through the fog of my twilight sleep is the two incredible trees standing majestically in their dualistic glory.

Chapter 4

I wake in the morning filled with dreams about my upcoming day with the trees. *What will it be like to be there again? Will it feel the same, or does it change by the day? And what do the trees smell like?* Try as I may, I can't access the memory of their scent, the only imprint that remains in my mind is the feeling of their power as it surged through my body, and the drop of my heart when we had to leave. I am certain that I could guess what they taste like based upon the way they smell; the scents of all of the other fruits hint at their flavor. Another thing that I couldn't figure was the absence of birds within their branches. If I were a bird, there is no other place that I would want to be. If I could fly, I would make a home in the highest branches in each and flit from tree to tree.

Adam still sleeps. Impatient for my adventure to begin, I wake him by jumping up and down on our bed. "Wake up! Wake up! Up and Adam!" I call, the sweetness of the morning fills me with life.

"No…" Adam groans, squinting one eye open and pulling me back into the bed beside him. "The sun has barely risen Eve, it's time to sleep."

I jostle his body side to side, "Come on. Let's go. Please?"

Adam doesn't move. He lies perfectly still, trying to reclaim his previous state of sleep.

"Please, Please, Please, Pleeeease?" I beg.

"Eve, sleep please. We'll go soon. I promise. Just sleep a little longer." He captures my head and traps it to his shoulder with his palm, patting my hair lovingly.

I sigh heavily in a show of surrender and settle back into the crook of his arm, "Okay."

I cross my arms over my chest and huff. He doesn't take notice of my embellished displeasure. I lay there quietly, scheming new ways to get him up. Inspiration hits. I tickle his nose and ears with the tips of my long hair, but he doesn't budge. He halfheartedly swats my hand, as if it is an insect with its flight too near. I pinch his nose and kiss his cheeks. I lick the entire length of his face.

That worked.

"Eve! Ugh. Okay, I'm up." Bolting up to a sitting position, he wipes the moisture from his face. "Let's go," he sighs, as if I am truly putting him out. He looks at me through half closed lids and yawns. "Did you prepare any food for us to take?"

I bite my lip, "Was I supposed to?"

Adam smiles as if he had just won a grand prize. Shooing me with his hand he dictates the first order of the day, "You go, prepare some food for us to take - *and I'll sleep just a little longer*." He flops back, a satisfied look of triumph on his face.

"I'll prepare it, but you'd better be ready to go when I get back."

"Mmm-hmm," Adam half mumbles, half yawns.

With a new lightness to my step I make my way to the garden outside of our home and pick an assortment of vegetables for lunch.

****

"Shhhhh." Adam eyes me seriously. "Look," he whispers, pointing to the north side of the lake.

There is a lioness drinking from the waters of the pool. Adam backs up, one step at a time, motioning for me to retreat to the tree line from where we came. Once tucked into the safety of the orchard Adam whispers, "Stay right here. Don't move."

Fearing his shift in mood, I question, "Why, what's going on?"

Adam moves along the edge of the trees, "Just stay here. Promise me?" he whispers urgently.

"I promise," I vow, holding my breath.

Adam disappears from my sight. I stand awkwardly, not knowing exactly what I should be doing. My heart quickens, eyes take in every detail of my surroundings, body primed to run at a moment's notice. I perceive a rustle within the trees on the north edge of the lake. I think I see Adam's crop of brown curls, but I can't be sure. I lean forward, on my toes. My heart stops when Adam springs from the foliage and ambushes the lioness, his arms secured around her neck.

I almost jump out of my skin when the lioness responds to the attack by roaring fiercely. She twists to free herself from his grip. Her thrashes are successful, Adam is thrown onto his back. The lioness crouches over him, stance dominant, broad face only inches from his. Her loud roar fills the land with the sound of her displeasure, her breath blows Adam's curls from his face. Adam scowls and growls back at her. The two stare at each other in a play for dominance. Adam pushes her face with one hand, and laughs, "Stop taking yourself so *seriously,* pretty girl!" He pushes her up, lifts her by her chest and tosses her over to his side. Scrambling to his feet, he leaps toward her as she tries to get away. Catching her by the backside, he holds her long tail for leverage and pulls himself to her shoulders fistful by fistful of her luxurious coat.

Once positioned on her back he lies his head down and nuzzles her neck, petting her roughly behind the ears. She again thrashes, a little gentler this time, jostling Adam from his place of dominance. Laughing, Adam slides down her side and rubs her jaw.

Irked, the lioness turns her head and licks her paw, making her displeasure with Adam's game apparent by giving him the cold shoulder. Adam howls with laughter,

"What is it with you girls today?" He ruffles the fur on her head, "None of you can take a joke."

The lioness responds to his easy tone, she softens and nuzzles his hand, purring.

"That's better," he says, scrubbing her neck. She basks under the glow of his attention. "Eve!" Come here, she's beautiful!"

I jog along the beach to meet Adam and his new friend.

"Here, pet her like this," Adam says, demonstrating how to scratch her behind the ears. Her flesh feels solid beneath my fingertips. She doesn't push against my palm as she had Adam's, in fact, her entire attention is focused on him. She nuzzles his neck with her nose and licks his face, which makes him yelp, "Ow! Yikes, your tongue is rough, pretty girl." He pulls his face back and maneuvers away from the creature's massive face. "Do you want to come play with us?" he asks, rubbing under her jaw. He turns toward me, "Are you ready to go to the clearing?"

The clearing. My heartbeat quickens, excitement circulates through my body.

"Yes." I can feel my eyes spark with interest.

"We can eat under the trees," he says, standing to stretch his body. He offers a hand, pulling me to my feet.

The energy in my body shifts as we approach the clearing. A silent celestial breeze blows through my very being, clearing it of everything but the life that animates it. When I see the trees again, my breath catches. They are even more majestic than I remember.

We step over the threshold, mere feet from my glorious universal altars. I am both mystified and contented by their presence.

"Eve, Look," Adam says, pointing to the lioness. She has halted at the line that separates the orchard from the clearing, laying so that her paws didn't cross the edge of the grass that surrounds the circular expanse of land. "Come here, girl," Adam calls. She doesn't heed his call, instead she bows her head, resting her nose on her paws. "Come here, girl!" he calls again, with more authority. The lioness whines, shifting her body uncomfortably – as if she wants to follow his order, but is compelled to follow a higher, instinctual authority to remain outside the border of the clearing.

"Why isn't she following your command?" I ask.

"I don't think she can," he responds, thoughtfully. "Maybe we are the only ones allowed to come here."

"Well, that explains why there are no birds in the branches," I breathe, fascinated. "I haven't even seen one fly above the clearing, they just circle around it," I say, point to the sky to demonstrate my point. A flock of birds skim a perfect circle along the edge of the tree line. "Which makes me wonder; why are *we* able to come inside?" Everything in this garden made perfect intuitive sense; except for the trees.

Adam comes close behind me, taking my shoulders in his warm hands, "This is our garden, Eve. We're allowed to go anywhere within it." Currents of warm and cool energy dance along the front surface of my body. The warm energy from The Tree of Life, and the cool from the Tree of the Knowledge of Good and Evil. They circulate in a perfect dance, each beautiful in its own way, each captivating my full attention. The Pandora fruit sparkles and twinkles, hinting at the mystery that it holds within. The fruit on the Tree of Life emits an audible hum and glows like a thousand midday suns, the golden embroidery on the solid white trunk of the tree weaving a pictorial tale.

Adam and I savor our meal. Famished, I eat with abandon. The flavors of the food are brought to life in a way that I have not experienced before. I can't get enough, yet I am deeply satisfied with each bite. Our meal comes to an end, not by choice, but because we have gone through our supplies. I lick the last juices of a strawberry from my fingertips and fall back into Adams arms. He strokes my shoulder and collarbone in lazy waves. Dazed by the trees, the meal, and the company, I am at rest. Yet, somewhere in my mind the mysteries of the trees still linger.

"Adam?" I ask.

"Hmmmm?" he replies, the relaxation in his voice soothes me.

"Where did all of this come from? The garden, the animals, us?"

Adam opens his mouth to answer, but before he can speak a boom of light sprays around us, dancing like swarms of fireflies in the sky, pouring from The Tree of Life in a shower of light. Startled, we jump to a sitting position and look to the tree in wordless surprise. The golden embroidery on the trunk pulls to one condensed point of light; then with an audible boom expands into a bright starburst of fire that causes us to shield our eyes. The golden thread begins to weave into form. We watch the pictorial tale of creation unfold in front of our eyes. The Earth forms; rotates around the sun. Stars and planets come into view as they spray around the canvas of the Tree of Life; they also orbit the bright sun in the center.

On the Earth, large masses of land rise from the ocean, the land blossoms, trees and foliage form, Adam's form raises from the Earth. Life is breathed into him and he stands, exploring the land around him. The story unfolds in warm gold tones. Adam and I lock eyes.

"Eve," Adam breathes in disbelief. "Eve, everything we just saw, the part about my first day in the garden, that all happened, exactly as it was shown..." he finishes, a look of awe on his beautiful face.

"Really?" I sit forward, my interest piqued.

We both look to the tree again.

"Ask it another question," I say, my throat tight.

"Ummmm," Adam scans his mind for a question, any question. "I can't think of anything to ask."

With haste, I think of an adequate one. "Tree: Where is the Creator, right now?"

The picture transforms, first the blinding sun. Then the Tree of Life. Then Adam and I lying beneath the tree, our chest illuminated with a golden light. I look to Adam. He shrugs his shoulders.

"Try another one," he suggests.

"Tree of Life: Why were we created?"

Again the scene before us transforms. Adam and I walk through the garden; we hold each other in a loving embrace. We dance, we laugh, we play. The scene ends.

34

"Whooa," I breathe, sitting back in disbelief. The tree, it seems to answer our questions. "Let's ask another one," the haste in my voice rises a degree.

Adam looks at me blankly, then smiles. "I can't think of anything to ask."

"There isn't one thing that you have been wondering about this place, or its purpose?"

"Honestly, no…" he replies.

Rolling my eyes I turn back to the tree, thinking. "Oh!" I exclaim. "I've got one! Tree of Life: Why are you and the Tree of the Knowledge of Good and Evil in the garden?"

A scene expands, The Tree of Life radiates, the garden blossoms into life. The animals play, the land produces vegetation and fruit. Adam and I commune under its branches, our every need met. The Tree of the Knowledge of Good and Evil expands into view, it absorbs the light of the Tree of Life, diluting everything around it. The vegetation in its proximity dulls, but the Tree of Life's power extends out bringing the withered vegetation back to life in a continuous cycle.

"What do you think that means?" I ask, even more enthralled.

"I don't know," Adam answers plainly. "But I think that you think too much. Where do all of these questions come from?"

"It is just so strange! I wish I understood its answers."

Adam brightens, an idea occurs to him, "Tree of Life: What should we do now?"

Our home is embroidered into the large white trunk, the scene enters our home. Adam and I are cuddled into our bed. Adam laughs,

"That tree just read my mind!" He draws me near, "I'm exhausted, let's go."

"Ohhhh," I whine. "Not yet."

"You heard the tree. It's time to sleep," he says. "Besides, the sun is about to set. Trust me, we don't want to get lost in the dark."

"Alright," I concede, rising to my feet in compliance. "But I want to come back tomorrow. Would that be okay?"

"Sure. I don't think that I'll come though, it's kind of boring just lying around. It makes me tired."

I ruffle his hair. "What are you going to do that is more interesting than *this*?"

"Anything," Adam answers. "I'd rather move, explore, use my body in some useful way. I don't like to just sit and do nothing."

"Okay, okay. You don't have to entertain me *all* of the time," I huff, rolling my eyes. "I'll be just fine without you."

He captures me from behind, pinning my arms to my side and spinning me to face him. "Ha! Victory!" he voices triumphantly, setting me back down on the ground. "Come on, daylight is almost gone." He kisses the tip of my nose and takes my hand.

I'm not ready to leave, my only consolation the catalogue of questions that I will ask the Tree of Life in the morning. When my foot crosses the threshold the cells in my body immediately begin to downgrade. I imagine living here, under the trees. Moving our home and never having to leave their magic again. The lioness rises from her post and follows us. As I close the door, I peek out to find her settling in for the night outside of the entrance of our home, as if on guard. She is acting strangely out of character for an animal of the garden. None have taken an interest in us before; they are usually content to go about their business. When she sees me spying on her, she growls a low warning. *How strange*, I muse as I close the door.

Chapter 5

"Adam?" I turn my head, the moon's light caresses his face with its subtle hue. Of course, he is asleep. I can't figure out how he does that. The moment he lay his head down, he drifts sweetly to sleep… while I lay there dreaming of the dualistic trees. I wonder why one shone in silver and one in gold? Why one was hot and the other cool to the touch? What was each one for, what purpose do they serve? Why does the Creator have two seemingly opposite trees? I wonder what they tasted like. I know that I will never know, but I am curious anyway. I resolve to ask the Creator to answer all of my questions about his beautiful trees when I meet him. I can't wait to find out.

****

At dawn, the first thought in my mind is the trees. Adam is still asleep beside me. I kiss him goodbye, careful not to rouse him. I have decided to venture to the clearing and come back before he wakes up. This is my favorite place in the entire garden. I feel the presence of the Creator there. My body feels different somehow; my senses become more acute and my mind clearer in the proximity of these exotic trees.

I anticipate the symphony as I approach the clearing. Instead, I hear something very different. The most glorious song that I have ever heard lilts through the air. Each note strikes a chord within me; chills spark the hairs along the entire length of my body. Excitement overtakes me. *The Creator.* My pace quickens to a run. *He's here.* I pause uncertainly, *Should I get Adam?* I don't want him to miss this but I don't know how long the Creator will be here. *What if I go back to get Adam only to return and miss meeting our Creator?* No, I will find the Creator first and bring Him to Adam.

As I near the clearing the song comes to an abrupt halt. A tall figure in green flowing robes makes a hurried departure. Anxiety, anticipation and the fear of a missed encounter blend into a tortuous overload of emotions that causes me to call out;

"Stop!" The word echoes and reverberates through the clearing back to my ears. *How odd, I have never heard my voice return to me in this way.*

The creature stops in his tracks, its broad shoulders stiffen. When this creature turns around I know that this is not the Creator, yet I am still intrigued. He looks like a man, but is far more glorious. Eight feet tall, long dark hair tied in a low knot at the nape of his neck. His cheekbones prominent, squared jaw, gently arched brows that frame his eyes. The proportions of his face harmonize grace, beauty and strength into one perfect canvas. His skin is pale and silvery, as if the moon shines directly upon it, though it is the middle of the day. He has a luminous iridescent pattern etched silently into his skin. I step closer and look into the creature's eyes. They are black, like onyx, and exotic. I feel dizzy. I have the sense that I am peering into the depths of eternity. It is a disorienting sensation that draws deeper. We stare for a long moment without speaking. It is I who breaks the silence, "What are you?"

The tall creature replies, "I am Lucas."

Another moment of silence passes.

"Lucas," I whisper to myself.

There is something about him. I feel as if I know him, as if I have known him for ages, though that is impossible as I was created only a short time ago.

"Do you live in the garden?" I ask.

Lucas offers his hand. The movement is as graceful as the bow of a fawn. I place my hand in his and my body is engulfed in a blanket of heat. I feel strange, intoxicated, good, I think, but I'm not sure. I am intrigued. I have never been so affected by anything… not even the trees. I feel a comfort around Adam, a love, an affection, but this all-encompassing sensation is new.

He takes my hand, leading me through the far west edge of the orchard to the body of water. I am confused. I crane my neck to look up at this glorious creature, two heads above mine and ask, "Do you live in the water?"

Lucas smiles, shakes his head and points to the surface of the water, "Look."

I look down and see Lucas in the water. I look closer. I don't understand. He was just behind me.

"How did you do that?" I speak breathlessly into the water. My fingertips reach forward to touch his face; ripples distort the lines of this gorgeous figure. Disturbed, I pull back my hand.

Lucas bursts into laughter, "Eve!"

Hearing his voice behind me startles me into a reflexive jump. I look back and he is there. He laughs, eyes shining, tears gathering in their corners. He looks at me as if I am precious. I look to the water; he is there. I look behind me; he is there. I smile, having just figured out this game.

"That is my reflection, Eve," he explains. "That is the magic of water. *Remember that, there is magic in the water.* Look…" He points toward the water again, and I see it: Me.

I am beautiful. My hair is the color of the amber sunset; it falls in smooth waves around my shoulders. My skin is pale and has the peach glow of health. Clear and smooth; it carries none of the patterns that Lucas has etched on his. My face is round and I have high rounded arches in my eyebrows. The delicate set of my lips frames perfect porcelain teeth. A small play of freckles splays across my nose. My eyes are green and deep. I am fascinated and can hardly look away. I have now found my second favorite thing in the garden. Behind me Lucas looks on approvingly.

"You are quite beautiful. I helped construct you, you know," he says pointing to the splay of freckles. "These were my idea. A thousand stars that glimmer across the face of the eve." He tugs my long silken strands, "And this was my idea, too. A crown of glory that glows as the setting sun. You know, that is why you are named Eve. That was always your name, even before it was given to you. *You are an evening beauty. Your beauty epitomizes the wonder of the setting sun. It is you who welcomes the night in all of its mysterious splendor.*" He strokes my hair with the lightest touch.

"Who are you?" I turn, a million questions in my eyes.

"I am an ancient one, one of the gods of heaven."

"Gods?" I ask. "I thought there is only one. Only one Creator."

"There is only one Creator, but I helped him create his creation. I, and another, helped the Creator design this place," he gestures around us, "and you as well."

I cannot help but look deep into his eyes. There is such comfort there, such mystery. "How?"

"There is much to tell you, my dear. But you must return to Adam. He waits for you. The sun is descending, my Eve."

I realize how long I have been away. *How is it possible that I have been gone all day?* I feel like I just left my house. I am confounded by the impossibility of it. "Oh, I do have to go," I

explain, a vague panic envelopes me. I left before Adam woke up, and now the sun is about to set and I still have not returned. Lucas' face drifts back into my mind, quieting all inner dialogue. Throwing a smile over my shoulder I look back and call,
"Lucas, meet me here tomorrow when the sun is at its highest."

Chapter 6
Present Day

Two things happen simultaneously at the realization of my dinner companion's identity. First, my body prickles as I feel myself being transported to an indefinable dimension, half a dimension away from where I was before. Second, the quality of the air changes from the subtle flow of life to absolute stillness.

Lucas. Here. Now. No.

My heart stops. I struggle to breathe.

No. No. No. No.

How could I have not recognized him? Maybe I did. If I was honest, he did seem familiar; maybe I mistook that familiarity for attraction: attraction that I haven't felt since my days in the garden. On some level I must have known, but blinded myself, indulging the possibility that I'd met another human who interested me, excited me to my very core. Maybe I denied what I knew in my bones because it has been so long since I have felt such hope, so alive. But there was no hope, for Evan was not human. He was - well, the devil.

I mentally explore a thousand possible things to say in this moment. I want to hurt him. Hurl my body at him; scratch out his eyes. I want to scream, hit, fight, tear the flesh from his bones. I want to walk away without a word. Deny him. I want to ask him *why.* I want to cry. I want to do so many things, but I just sit there in shock, dumb, looking blankly into his face.

I stand. The chair behind me crashes to the ground. My heart races. My head feels light. Knees weak. I feel the traces of a fainting spell being cast over me. I grab the table for support and lean forward to look into his eyes. Yes, now I can see. Those eyes I recognize. Deep and bewitching. Is it possible that they now hold something else? What could it be? Regret? Pain? Anguish? Hope? I couldn't tell, but they have changed. We both hold our breath, waiting for the other to speak.

What can I say? There is too much to be said, too many conflicting emotions, so I keep my silence. I wait to hear what the devil has to say to me the first time that we have spoken since betraying me.

Nothing. He just looks at me with tormented eyes. Why doesn't he speak?

I back away from him, edging toward the door.

"Eve," he says my name carefully.

An unseen force carries me backward. I float rather than walk. I know that I am using my feet, but I don't feel them beneath me. This doesn't feel real. He stands, striding toward me. He touches my arm, "Eve. Wait. Don't go."

A rush of fury washes over me. Every cell in my body catches fire; my throat burns with words that I have been waiting to utter for thousands of years. "Do. Not. Touch. Me," I warn, with the menace of a hundred war-time blades.

He does not pull back; he moves his hands to my shoulders.

"I said don't touch me!" I scream, writhing from his hold. Floodgates release as my shock abates. A primal scream escapes my lips. I hit him. Violence streams unbounded from me as I release an eternity of anger that I have not fully acknowledged or let myself feel, the rage that I have carried in my heart for all of this time. This rage has heavied every step that I have taken, edged every smile I have given, bound every moment that I wished to be free.

"I hate you. You incredible bastard. I hate you!" My fury turns to tears, inconsolable sobs. "You used me. You lied to me. You ruined my life. You ruined my life… you ruined my life… you ruined everything…" I repeat over and over again, still beating his chest. I'm frustrated that my physical capacity for destruction pales in comparison to what I wish I could do to him. If I could, I would break him in two. Using all of my strength I deliver one final blow.

Lucas does nothing, he just stands there.

"Say something!" I scream, my lungs burning. "Say something!"

"I'm sorry," he says, eyes searching.

"You're sorry? That's it? That's all you have to say for yourself? After everything that you have done - all you have to say for yourself is *you are sorry*? Why are you here, Lucas?"

I push him away, he yields.

"I'm sorry that I've hurt you." He eyes me with tender regret.

"That's it? What about everything and everyone else? What about the billions of others that you have tormented within an inch of their lives? What about the planet? What about Adam? You know what… forget it. There's nothing that you can say that will make up for what you've done. They are just words, Lucas… You can't just say that you're sorry… it doesn't change anything," an unfamiliar coldness, hard as steel, edges my voice. "If you try and find me again I will kill you."

"Eve. We have to talk. You have to listen to what I have to say. Just wait. You must understand how difficult it was for me to come to you. Please, just listen to me," he begs.

"No. Not now, not ever. You are unbelievable… pretending to want to save the world. Lying to me, drawing me in, only to betray me again? Go to hell. *Oh wait, we are already there, because of you!* Leave me alone, Lucas. I will never, ever, forgive you." I run toward the door, expecting to fight Lucas off. He does not follow me.

When my feet cross the threshold of the private dining room into the restaurant I see why we were not disturbed during our confrontation. Lucas has taken us out of time. A hundred diners are frozen, each in the perfect pose of the New York dining experience. It looks like a magazine advertisement. Smiles, drinks toasting, jovial diners-mid laugh. I do not stop; I run outside into the snow, each flake suspended in the air. Everywhere that I look the motion of human existence has ceased. Life has stilled to a halt. Each inhabitant holds the posture of the exact moment that I realized who sat across the table from me.

I run.

Back to the office.

Past motionless coworkers.

Keys. I need my keys.

I riffle through my purse.

Garage.

Start car.

I drive through the parking garage barrier, onto the street.

Cars litter the street, I cannot pass.

Pedestrians, like statues on the sidewalk. I cannot pass.

Nowhere to go.

I leave my car.

Nowhere to go.

Hotel.

Steal room key.

Fall on bed.

Lay dumbly in shock.
Paranoia sets in. I feel him coming for me.
I imagine him inches away from my door.
I call to God silently in my head.
It is only a matter of time.

Chapter 7
The Beginning

I return to Adam, cheeks flushed, eyes bright with excitement. Adam is delighted,

"Eve! What's happened? You look radiant!"

"Oh, Adam, I have had the most wonderful day, I met…" I hesitate, "I met the most beautiful, err, the most beautiful *field of flowers*. They were absolutely enchanting!" I smile, hoping that he didn't notice my awkwardness.

He casts a sideways glance, "Eve. Really? Trees sing to you? Flowers enchant you?" He shakes his head, "I will never understand."

I ruffle his hair, "Adam, you spend all day with the animals, playing, hiding stalking. I will never understand that!"

I have never hidden anything from Adam before, but I'm not ready to share my meeting Lucas yet. I want to spend a little more time with him before I have to share. I don't want Lucas' attention divided. I adore his conversation and am not ready to have the experience of that diluted. Adam will meet him, but perhaps I can spend a little more time with him first. *That's not so wrong, is it?*

As night descends we settle in and gaze at the moon, crickets chirp their song all around. My thoughts return to the Creator's trees, Lucas, and the mystery that I feel will soon be revealed. I had never heard of any other creatures besides man, animal, or the Creator before. I turn to Adam,

"Where does the Creator live?" I ask. "Why doesn't he live here, in the garden with us?"

Adam considers my question, "I'm not sure. I've never met him. But someday we will, and we can ask him then."

"How do you know he exists, if you have never met him?"

"I can feel him, here." He points to his chest. "I can feel his love in every part of my body, and most of all, I can see him right here." He touches the tip of my nose with his finger.

"How can you see him in my face, if you've never seen his face before?"

Adam sighs, "Eve, I've been in the garden longer than you. I came alive just as you did, but when I woke up I was alone. I did everything by myself. I explored the garden, made friends with the animals, tasted the fruits of the trees and vegetables of the land. I swam, I whistled, I sang, I hopped, I jumped off of rocks and cliffs, I ran, I played, and I built this," he finishes his catalogue, motioning to our shelter. "I was in paradise, but felt there was something missing.

"One night, I went for a walk and got lost. It was dark, and I couldn't find my way back home. There were no animals around, just me. I couldn't get my bearings; the only thing that I knew was that I was walking in circles. There was this haze of light in the distance... it looked as if a piece of the sun had fallen to the earth and was lighting the land. I followed the light and I found the clearing for the first time, only, there was just one tree. The Tree of Life. I sat there for a long time, just looking at the tree. I'd never seen anything like it. I knew that the fruit was not mine to eat. Honoring that knowing, and I don't know why I did this, but I acknowledged it out loud, making a vow that I would never taste its fruit.

Then I felt it. *The Creator*. I felt him fill me with love. I can't describe it. You think that the trees are powerful, because that is all that you have felt, but this filled me to my very core. It was that type of communion that I had been longing for. I knew that the Creator was there, that he was listening, so I asked for a companion to create the same type of feeling with. That's the last thing I remember. I fell asleep and when I woke up you were there, beside me. I was shocked that it was so immediate. You were the most beautiful thing I had ever seen. I felt complete. You were mine, and I was yours. You were everything that I had been missing. I felt the same love *for you* that the Creator had expressed for me the night before. You didn't wake up right away. It was getting dark again, so I lifted you, to take you home. I looked toward the Master's tree, I guess to thank Him, and I saw there was now another tree beside it. The tree whispered its name to me, *The Tree of the Knowledge of Good and Evil*. Dread filled me and I knew that this tree was not to be eaten of either. It struck a chord of fear in me. I vowed not to eat the fruit of The Tree of Life out of respect for the Creator. I now vowed not to eat of the fruit of The Tree of the Knowledge of Good and Evil from a place of fear. I don't know how I know, but I know." He smiled, "and that is *how I know, that I know, that I know* the Creator."

I am moved by Adam's story. This was a side of himself that he had not shown me before. This has been a very unusual day. Lost in

46

thought, I turn to my side and mull over all that had been revealed to me, trying to put the pieces together. I felt that if I somehow could, I would know my Creator. I resolved to find out as much as I could tomorrow when I returned to Lucas.

****

I awake the in the morning with great excitement. All morning my heart sings. I can't wait until the hour that I will see Lucas again. I am filled with an exuberance that I have not known before. The closer the sun comes to the high point in the sky, the faster my heart beats. I tell Adam that I'll be back after a while and make my departure. I can't wait to see Lucas.

I run to the pond where I left him last. My skin buzzes with anticipation. Lucas sits by the water. My heart skips when I see him. He is even more luminous than I remembered. His dark eyes light up when he sees me. Smiling widely, a big, bright, warm smile, he stands and opens his arms for a hug,

"Eve!" he calls, as if he were just as happy to see me.

Hugging him holds such a natural sensation. I feel as if my body were being transported, to where I don't know, but it is disorienting in the best possible way. We rest in our embrace for a long time, wrapping ourselves in the engulfing love that pours from our hearts.

"Eve," he pulls back to look at me. "Eve, how do you feel today?"

His smile, it was one that I could not resist. It was infectious. Shyly I respond,

"I feel wonderful. I've been thinking about you. I have so many questions."

"Come, sit." Lucas motions to the place where he had been sitting. "Sit like this," Lucas says, crossing one leg over the other rocking his hips side to side. Obediently I bend one leg over the other and pull my foot through.

"How does that feel?" he asks.

"Awkward." I laugh.

"Rock your hips side to side like this, and straighten your spine."

I follow his instructions.

"This is called Lotus."

"Like the flower?"

"Very perceptive," Lucas' voice gleams with admiration. "It's called that because as you practice sitting like this, the top of your head opens like a lotus flower."

Laughing I ask, "What *are* you talking about?"

Lucas takes my hands, "Let me show you, close your eyes."

Obeying, I close my eyes.

"Now, relax your shoulders. Breathe in and out. Feel your palms, feel the warmth of my palms on yours." An energy engulfs my body, a fluid delicious energy. My body feels weightless, breath becomes deep and effortless. I feel my mind open. The boundaries of my body fade, and I can feel the space around me, as if my body were the space. I can feel Lucas; a bright energy emanates from him and merges with mine. He and I are one, as I am one with everything around me. I can feel the life in the grass beneath us, perceive the air around my body as a living, breathing entity. I am one, transported to the cosmos. I feel the simple vastness of the Universe. We are beyond time.

A circular sensation stirs at the crown of my head. An opening; it feels like the top of my head is opening; like a lotus blooming. *Lucas was right,* as the thought enters my mind, something snaps. I am back in my body, a separate being again.

I open my eyes. Everything looks softer somehow, more vibrant. Lucas smiles.

"What was that? How did you do that?" I ask, feeling my eyes widen in wonder.

"You just experienced a moment of evolution."

"Evolution?" I ask. "What's that?"

"Evolution is growth past what you knew you were capable of. You have been given life to evolve, and become like me. This is your purpose, Eve." Still looking deeply into my eyes, something mysterious happens; somehow an essential truth passes through his eyes into mine, an essential truth that is deeper than his words; *an essential truth that needed no words.*

"Your life, here in this garden, can be about more than just mere enjoyment. It can be a life where you challenge yourself. You felt a moment of that, just now, didn't you? What was it like?" he asked, squeezing my hands in gentle encouragement.

A sheepish smile passes my lips, eyes cast to the ground. For some strange reason, I feel bashful about sharing my experience, "I don't know how to put it into words."

"Try," he encourages.

I close my eyes and try to remember the fleeting moment, "I felt the life in the ground, and the air. Then I felt the life in *me* merge with the life in *it*. My mind opened and I saw stars and wide space and felt how time and space are one." Embarrassed, I didn't mention how brightly he shone, or how wonderful it felt to merge my energy with his. I open my eyes and look at him in hopeful anticipation.

Obviously proud of my astute observations; he praises me, "Very, very good, Eve. Can I ask, what brought you back, here, into this body, back into time?"

I tried to remember, *what was it?* I contemplate for many moments, finally shaking my head, "I can't recall."

Lucas urges on, "Did you feel something in your body that brought your attention back to it? Did you have a thought?"

"*I had a thought*. I remembered what you said about the Lotus blooming from the top of my head; I felt it. I felt the top of my head open like a Lotus blossom!"

He laughs, "That's it. With that one thought you were pulled out of the moment. You gave up the state of *all thought* to focus your attention on *one thought*. An evaluation and identification with a moment that happened in the past. You must learn to let go of individual thoughts in order to achieve the oneness of the gods. A mind that narrates and evaluates is a mind that is singular. A mind that observes and accepts is vast. Do not attach yourself to anything Eve."

Lucas motions to the body of water that we sit near, "Let your mind be free, like the lotus that grows on the surface of the water; beautiful, alive, but not rooted."

In that moment something shifts. It is tangible, yet indefinable. An interchange of trust and love passes between us. *Does he notice?* Something definitely has shifted. I've accepted something unspoken from him. He does notice; in response he pulls me into a hug and holds me. Resting my body against his, allowing myself to yield to the embrace, I again feel the vastness of the universe and eternity.

****

"Can I show you something?" Lucas asks, casting his chin downward, raising his perfectly arched brows.

Delighted, I cannot wait to see what it is, "Of course!"

The whisper of a thrill twists up my spine extending upward with each second that passes, stacking each vertebrae into perfect order. A look of single-minded focus sets upon his features. He's the most handsome when he concentrates; brows pulled, eyes intent, mouth set in a perfect bow. He purses his lips, almost as if he is going to kiss someone, or something, drawing them inward while he focuses on the task at hand. Every time this expression crosses his face, I cannot help but stare in fascination at his particularly breathtaking beauty. He dips his hand in the crystal body of water of the shore that we sit upon. An orb of water begins to take form in his palm, the edges of which congeal, responding to his will. He raises his hand and holds his creation proudly; a six-inch orb floats inches above his palm, his intent gaze reflected through the bubble of water. Delighted by his show of magic I gasp in awe,

"How did you do that?" I reach my finger to touch the orb. When my finger depresses the gelatinous surface the bubble bursts, spraying water over the both of us. Surprised and soaked, we both laugh. We laugh far harder than the occasion demands, but there is an anticipatory relief in that moment. Tears of delight touch our eyes. "Do it again! Please?" I plead.

Lucas' eyes twinkle. Showing off a bit now, he gathers another orb of water. The bubble rests in the air above his hand, his eyes focused, he changes the color of the bubble. A transparent shield of red forms over the surface of the orb. It turns to orange, then yellow, green, blue, and at last, indigo. The orb holds the rainbow in perfect shows of color.

"Hold out your hand," Lucas instructs.

The orb floats through the distance between us and stops to rest in the space above my palm. It buoys above my hand subtly, an invisible force beneath it. Invisible, but real.

My mind begins a rampage of questions: *Where did this invisible force come from? Why have I never felt it before? Am I making this happen or is Lucas? Why can I not see it? What is this force made of?*

Lucas interrupts this indulgence of thought, directing me to concentrate, "Focus on the orb. Use your eyes to connect your attention with the water."

I refocus, just as he had asked.

"Now use your mind to change its color. Connect with each drop of water in the orb and use your will to bend the light within it. All colors already exist within this orb, just choose the one that you would like and augment. Don't tell me what the color is. I want you to know for certain that it is you who has the power to transform matter," he says.

I concentrate on the now crystalline orb. The shade turns to a transparent, washed out, orange, the color of which was almost imperceptible.

"Eve, that is excellent for your first time! Keep focusing," he coaches.

My brain strains so hard that I can now hear my heartbeat thud its constant rhythm in my ears. Instead of having my full attention on the orb in front of me, it keeps being drawn to the thud, thud, thud of my heart. Surprisingly, the circumference of the orb vibrates with each beat. Lucas laughs,

"Eve, where is your focus?"

"My heartbeat."

He laughs again, "Alright, it looks like you have hit your capacity on this for today. Pass it back to me. To do this you must use your mind to create positive space on the opposite side of the ball. Use that positive space to move the orb to me."

As my mind follows his instructions I begin perceive a resistant force between my body and the orb. At a painfully slow pace the bubble moves forward toward Lucas' upturned palm as I use all of my might to concentrate.

"Watch this," Lucas says. The orb of water solidifies into an opaque ball and falls into his hand with a heavy thump. He laughs and tosses the ball to me.

"It's cold!" I toss the weighty ball back into his hands.

"Watch this," Lucas spins the ball in his hands. "I'm going to make it disappear." The spinning ball transforms into the liquid orb, then vanishes into a puff of steam, and disappears into thin air. I jump up and down on my seat, unable to control my excitement. Taking in my enthusiasm, Lucas grabs my hands,

"I have much more to show you. Much more to teach you, but for now it is time for us to part. You must return to Adam, it's getting late."

My heart sinks with disappointment, "Just show me one more thing? Please?" I plead for more of his magic. I wish that I could extend the afternoon.

"How can I resist that face?" he laughs, tapping the tip of my nose with the pad of his finger. "Alright one more thing, then you *must* go."

I nod fervently in agreement, excited to see what magic was in store for me next.

"I will teach you how to create something out of nothing. What would you like to create?"

"Anything?"

"Anything."

"A rose!" I exclaim.

"Easy. Here, take my palms." Holding out his palms for mine, I place my hands in his and melt - the sensation much more than delightful. He is so amazing. I feel amazing when I am near him, he shows me amazing things, we talk about amazing things; amazing, amazing, amazing. I am amazed at his amazingness. He dissolves my mental altar to his awesomeness,

"Close your eyes. Follow my instructions with your mind," he says.

Dutifully, I obey.

"Feel the space above your head. Focus on the space above your head. Put your mind on the space above your head," he repeats his instructions to ensure that I follow. "You should feel a swirling sensation in the space above your crown. It feels like a small circular breeze, cool wisps of energy. Feel that energy enter your body through the crown, relax your mind as it passes. Clear your mind of all thought, feel the center of your brain. Clear all thought-except for the picture of your rose.

"Imagine it sprout, then grow, from the land between us. See the vibrant colors of the bud unfolding, its fragrant petals inviting with its heady scent. See the picture clearly, add any detail that you would like. See exactly how the rose will look, decide how you want the petals to curl. Decide how many thorns will cleat up the sides. Picture every detail that you want to create. Now, take that picture and let the image fall into the space of your throat. Let it rest there. Do not open your eyes.

Keep your mind on your picture say, out loud, *'I now grow a rose'*. When you do this see the form float from your lips into the space around you, preparing the land for your will."

"I now grow a rose," I say. I imagine first the air, then the land, accepting the imprint of that I want to create.

Lucas continues, "Allow the picture to descend from your throat into your heart. Feel your love for the rose, the gratitude that the rose has been created. Allow yourself to feel the love create a new depth and dimension - it's no longer just a picture; it now has form.

Now let the form of the rose pass into your upper abdomen. Determined, know with absolute certainty that the rose has been created. See the form fill out - into a plush rose. Know with absolute certainty that you are creating. Let the formed energy pass into your lower abdomen, the form takes density. Let the dense, formed energy fall to the base of your spine and allow it to sink into the Earth. Let go of all pictures that you have – let go of all energy that you have just created. Let it drift completely into the Earth, empty all of the energy from your body into the Earth and let your mind be blank. Do not hold onto a drop of that energy. Do not hold on to one expectation. To allow it to be created you must let it all go. It's no longer yours to hold. Give it to the Earth now."

I let it go. I feel my body empty. I feel a deep connection with the Earth as I pass my creation along to her. I feel the Earth open up and receive the creation from me.

"Now, open your eyes," he says.

I open my eyes. In the grass between Lucas and I grows a single fuchsia rose. Every vivid detail that I imagined is perfectly displayed within the form of this flower. My mind feels clear and free, my body warm with excitement. I am intoxicated with the process of creation. I feel a deep sense of accomplishment. *I made that happen.* I felt myself receive and transform the energy within my mind and body. I felt the Earth receive that energy and collaborate with me. It made perfect sense. Heaven, human, Earth. We all were co-Creators intended to work in perfect harmony. Heaven provided the energy, I turned it into form and the Earth made it a reality.

Lucas plucks the rose from the ground and smells it, closing his eyes to appreciate its clean scent. He opens his eyes and smiles, adjusts the stem to the proper height, places it behind my ear, "There you go. One more thing."

Chapter 8
Present Day

I awake from a dreamless stress-induced slumber. *How long have I been asleep?* My head aches. Looking around the hotel room that I had commandeered, I locate the phone. When I cradle it to my ear I discover that there is no dial tone. I walk to the window; outside things are just as they were when I entered. Motionless. *How long can this last? Had time stopped for the world, or just me?* Lucas had trapped me. I had nowhere to go. Life would not continue until I heard what he had to say. I was a hostage and there was no one to save me.

Resigned, I straighten the room, erasing all evidence of my intrusion. I gather my things slowly, prolonging the inevitable. When I open the door and look back into the room, I catch a glimpse of myself in the mirror. The same familiar face is reflected back to me. It is the very same face that I have had for all of my lives, but there is something different about this version – the expressionless stare that greets me tells a tale of continuous suffering. *Why is it always so hard? Why do I continually have to go through this?* I regret being born. I regret every moment that I have lived. *I consider giving up, killing myself, but I know that will not end the game. I will just be born again and again.* It's no use. There is no rest for me. I must face him, not because I want to, but because life never offered me any choice, it *never* did. I am bitter, because of this cruel joke called life. I hate it, but I have no other option. I will face Lucas because I must. I will convince him to give me up, give everything up.

A vague sense of determination prickles within me. I wish that my strength wasn't as subtle as it was; but it was a start. Taking a deep breath, feigning bravery, I close the door and descend the stairs. He is waiting for me, and the time has come to face him.

On the street, my face pushes the snowflakes in the path that I walk. They do not melt when they hit the warmth of my skin; instead, my face moves them like a shovel. Several times, after too many flakes had accumulated to see, I gather the mounds into a ball and push it to the side. When time unfroze, these snowballs would appear to have come from nowhere, falling at the feet of puzzled pedestrians. I thought of Adam, and smiled. Imagining the hundreds of pranks he would have delighted in, once upon a time when his soul was still young. I imagined his devious smile as he gathered mounds of snow above the heads of his unsuspecting victims. I imagine the exhilaration of a good prank gleam in his beautiful eyes. I miss him. I hope that wherever he is, he has found peace without me. I regret ever being his companion, as by just being myself, I made his life exceedingly difficult. The poor man never got any rest, because of my fate to attract the most bizarre situations. I hope that his experience of life without me has brought him the peace that he deserves.

Even after my lifetimes of experience I still can't figure if I am just unlucky or if there really is some unseen karmic balance that I have been obligated to pay. My belief in the former has given me the will to keep going - to keep attempting to pass unforeseen tests of my character; keeping my diligence trial after trial. But I wonder. *Is it luck? Am I just the unluckiest person in the history of humanity?* I couldn't have deserved this. Not from the beginning. I remember myself as a young soul, I was so pure, so full of love. I never would have hurt anyone, not the way that life has hurt me.

The world has gotten progressively darker, progressively more abusive. Admittedly I have hardened, lost hope – but that is in response to my environment. *I did not create the world, the world created me.* My will has been exhausted. I am tired. I don't know how much longer I can go on. As always, I will face the situation at hand. I will face Lucas, but I hope it is over soon. My exhaustion runs deep, to the bone. I don't have much more in me. The wandering of my mind ebbs when I enter the lobby of O.N.E. Earth. Everything here is in pristine order, the only sound the soft rustle of my clothes as I retrace my steps to the founder's office. I feel him. He is waiting for me.

Chapter 9
The Beginning

As I walk toward our home, I am completely engrossed in thought. Lucas' magic fills my mind. I replay the scene over, experiencing every moment once more, pouring over the details with exacting scrutiny. *How had he done all of those things? Had I preformed the magic or had Lucas only let me take part in the experience? Was it Lucas' power or had I learned to manipulate the forces of the Universe myself?* I hoped it was the latter.

It was time for Adam to meet Lucas. I am thrilled at the prospect of sharing this experience with him, showing him all of *my* mysteries of the garden, just as he had shown me his when I was first created.

"Adam!" I burst through the door.

"Adam?" I look around, all is quiet. I run outside.

"Adam!"

"Yeah?" His reply if muffled.

I look around but don't see him. "Where are you?"

"I'll be in, in a minute," he calls, his voice sounds strange, distant.

"Where *are* you?" I look around, curious.

Adam walks around the corner. "Why are you so late? Where were you?"

"I'm sorry. I was with someone, actually. That's why I called you when I arrived home, I want you to meet him."

Adam looks confused, "Him?"

"Yes, him. He is not human, but he looks like one. His name is Lucas, he is a heavenly creature, called an Angel," I explain. "That's what took me so long, he was showing me how to make roses *grow* and water *float*!" I say, my eyes gleam with the memory. "You must come with me tomorrow to meet him! You'll love him."

"Yeah?" Adam brightens. "An Angel, huh? What does he look like?"

"He looks a lot like us; two legs, two arms, face like ours, but he is tall, I mean *really* tall. His eyes are black, instead of brown or green like ours, and his skin, it's," I search for the word to describe his skin. "Well, you'll just have to see it."

"Does he know the Creator?" Adam asks.

"Yes, he does! He showed me in a meditation. I mean, I didn't see God, but I felt him. It was awesome!"

"Really?" Adam perks.

"Yes. I can't wait for you to meet him. He can show you the most amazing things, like today, he showed me how to make water float, *in the air*." My wide eyes punctuate the point.

"It's settled then! We shall go in the morning." Adam exclaims, taking my hand.

Chapter 10

"Lucas!" I call out as Adam and I approach the shore. I look around, everything is still. "Lucas!" I call again, louder this time. I look at Adam. "That's strange. I expected him to be here."

"Are you sure this is where we were supposed to meet him?"

"Yes, positive." *Where is he?* He has been here every day since the day we met, right here, by the water. My heart sinks. I peek through the tree line, though I know he isn't there. "I thought he would be here."

"That's okay. Maybe another day?" Adam tries to sound optimistic, but I can read the disappointment clearly on his face.

I sigh, disappointed, too. I walk toward the water's edge and sit. I pat the ground next to me, "Come, sit."

Adam settles in next to me. He closes his eyes and breathes the crisp, cool air deep into his lungs, leaning back to bask in the warmth of the sun.

"Here," I say, drawing Adam's attention. "I'll show you some of the things that Lucas taught me. Look here." I point toward the water, "Have you ever seen what you look like in the still water?"

Adam looks at the reflective surface. He smiles, then frowns, then makes an array of peculiar expressions, appraising the planes of his face. "I have, but I forgot how handsome I am." He smiles at his reflection.

"You've seen yourself before?" I ask, shocked. Seeing my reflection in the water was such an important moment for me. I almost can't believe that Adam didn't lead me to that experience, knowing that it existed.

"Just once. When I was diving into the pond. But I've never looked closely." Adam backtracks, sensing my alarm. He leans in toward his refection and scrutinizes the angles of his face in a display of appreciation for my efforts.

I sigh, "That's not all that I have to show you." I put my hand in the water, just as Lucas had. I make an effort to congeal the water into an orb. I try to clear my mind of all thought, but my thoughts keep returning to Adam's expectation. Frustrated, I shake my head side to side, shaking the thoughts off with the motion. I try again. *Water. Orb. Water. Orb.* Slowly, the water gathers and rests in an oblong shape in my palm. Not quite the orb I was aiming for, but a good start. I hold the flat shape in my hand and create an opposing magnetic force in the space beneath the water, raising it from my palm. It works. The water lifts one millimeter above the surface. I try to manipulate the shape into an orb. The edges of the formation quiver but do not budge. Excited, I look to Adam. As my attention is diverted - the water falls with a splash. I look up at Adam feeling particularly proud. He looks at me in wordless awe. I smile broadly. "Do you want to try?"

"Of course, I do!" Adam blurts.

"Okay," I instruct. "Place your hand in the water, palm facing up."

Adam follows my instruction.

"Now gather the water into your palm. Feel the water, feel the properties of the water. Focus on the water that has gathered in your hand. In your mind, picture it taking form. See it gelling, binding."

I watch as Adam naturally succeeds, as he always does. The water responds immediately. Feeling a tinge of jealousy at how easy this task is for him, I do not tell him to shape the water into an orb, as I am afraid that he will be able to do this with no trouble. This new feeling that springs within me surprises me; it shocks me that I do not want Adam to succeed more than I had. This emotion feels strange inside of my body and I do not like it.

To overcome this jealousy, I encourage Adam to do the very thing that I was opposed to moments ago, as it isn't my place to hold him back according to my own limitation. "Adam, use your mind shape the water into an orb."

As predicted, without hesitation the water takes shape. I nod my head, allowing my heart to be proud of him. "Very good, Adam! Your mind is so strong!" I say delighted that I was able to overcome my internal struggle. "I wasn't able to do that."

Adam bites his lip. He doesn't take his eyes from the orb that rests in his hand. His face looks a lot like Lucas' when he focuses. Brows drawn in, lips pursed. I wonder if I also make this same adorable face while concentrating.

"Alright, Adam. Now use your mind to float the water in space above your palm. Use your mind to create a negative charge under the sphere."

"What do you mean?" Adam asks; eyes still on the orb.

I think of another way to explain it, "Use your mind to create a negative force under the orb to push it upward."

"I don't know what you mean." Adam looks up. Right then the bubble loses its form and pours into his palm, formless once more. "Ha!" he laughed. "You can't take your eyes off the orb, can you?"

"No, you can't," I say, shaking my head affectionately.

"So I guess your Angel really is a no-show, huh?" he asks easily, wiping the moisture from his hands.

"I guess so," I sigh.

"Well, I'm glad that we came anyway. I appreciate what you taught me to do. I'll keep practicing and one day, I'll be able to lift this entire lake!"

"I don't doubt it," I answer. I really didn't, Adam could do anything.

****

"Where are you going?" Adam asks. He lounges in the common room of our home, a sliver of noonday sun peeks through the canopy, traveling in shining patterns across his face.

"For a walk," I answer, morosely.

"You're not still upset about your Angel being a no-show, are you?" he asks.

How could I deny it? I could hear the dullness of my voice, feel it in the slump of my shoulders, the heaviness of my step. "Yeah, I guess," I reply, unable to work up any enthusiasm.

"Eve, I had a great time." He kisses the top of my head. "I know you wanted me to meet him, and I will. We'll go back tomorrow"

My mood lifts a little at Adam's reassurance. "I know, I just wanted to share the experience of meeting an angel with you. You've shared so much with me and I was excited to finally be able to show you something."

"You did. I've never floated a ball of water in the air, and you didn't even need your Angel there to help you." He hugs me and nips my ear with his teeth, causing the hair on the back of my neck to stand on end. Prickles trickle up my spine. He jostles my body side to side as if he were trying to shake the melancholy out of me. It works. I giggle, the freshness returning to my spirit.

"You feel better?" he asks, looking into my eyes inquisitively.

"I need some air. I'm going for a walk, but I'll be back before dark, I promise." I plant a kiss on his cheek. "See you tonight."

My feet lead me past the clearing to the water's edge. To my surprise Lucas sits by the water weaving a wreath of flowers.

"Lucas! Where were you this morning?" I demand, accusation edges my voice. My disappointment was replaced by anger.

"I was here," he replies unruffled, a peaceful smile rests upon his face.

"No. You weren't. I came here with Adam and you were not here."

He finishes his wreath of white flowers, holds it back and appraises his work, looking upon it with satisfaction. Standing, he places the crown upon my head. "I was here. You just didn't see me."

Frustrated, I speak through gritted teeth, "*If you were here, and you saw that we were here, why didn't you come out?*"

Lucas laughs, the subtle notes of his laughter relax the rigidity of my stance. "I wanted to see how you and Adam interact. I was curious," he muses. "You were brilliant today, by the way." He laughs, "I was shocked that you were able to teach Adam how to manipulate the elements, on your first try. You are even more brilliant than I gave you credit for. You really are special." The affection shines through his eyes caressing every cell in my body. When he compliments me, he compliments me with more than just his words. I feel it in every level of my being. My body responds to his praise more than my mind. It comes to me as permeating waves of cool beauty.

"I still wish that you would have come out to meet him. He was really excited. It hurt me to disappoint him," I confess, in earnest.

"I know Eve. I could see it on your face. I wanted to come out from hiding, if only to ease your discomfort, but Eve, Adam isn't ready to meet me. Soon though, soon we will meet," he promises.

"What do you mean when you say that he isn't ready?" I ask.

Lucas takes my hands, "You are special Eve; that is why I come to you. That is why I teach you. *Our meeting was no accident; it was our destiny.* You are naturally able to understand things that Adam isn't ready to know. You'll have to be his teacher, Eve, just as I am yours. Today proved that to me, more than ever. You have a natural ability," he says proudly. "You're not still mad, are you?" he asks, disarming me with charm. "You understand why I couldn't come out just yet don't you?"

"Of course, I trust that you know what is best." I look at him with wide, open eyes.

"I'm glad that you came back. I've been here waiting for you. I have something that I want to show you." He dips his chin to look into my eyes. I get lost there. We stare silently, delicately reconnecting ourselves in preparation for our next lesson.

****

I sit with Lucas in meditation. We have merged our energy bodies and I am in a state of peace. Lucas begins to hum, his voice lilts through the air, blending with the strange melody of the trees. My consciousness drifts into a state of nothingness and I begin to dream of beautiful things that I do not understand.

I see a vision of Lucas. He has beautiful silver feathered wings that cast rays of white light from their tips, creating a majestic aura around him. His green robes rustle in an unseen breeze. He is singing. His clear voice pierces eternity. The depth of love that pours from his song shatters my heart with joy.

He is worshipping the Creator of all that is. Innocence and adoration shine like a light from his face, his focus is on the Creator powerful. Every thought that he has, every word that he utters, is in devotion to the Creator. In return, I can feel the Creator's love for Lucas pour into him, fueling his devotion further. The Creator's love is perfect, complete, and whole, there is no limit, the depths of which extend beyond my comprehension.

Lucas is filled with the light of the Creator. He shines from within, practically bursting with light, which he directly recycles back to the Creator. There is a seamless circuitry between the loved and the beloved. No other angel in heaven has developed the capacity to hold the amount of light that Lucas carries, as the amount of light each being holds is in direct relation to the amount of devotion. No other could possibly love the Creator more than Lucas and that is apparent just by looking at him.

As a result of this devotion, Lucas is the dearest and most beloved of the Creator. The more light Lucas receives, the deeper his devotion develops, the greater his capacity to love. He holds so much light that he is far brighter than all of those around him. Because of this he is celebrated by the others for his beauty, but that does not matter to him, he scarcely notices this fame, as his attention is not diverted from the Creator for even a moment. Lucas' being is so filled with the light of the Lord that he has *become* the light. The holiness, the wholeness, is something to behold.

I feel a shift. Something happens. The details of which I cannot access. Lucas' light dims, just a bit, then a little more. His singular focus has been diverted. I can see doubt in his face, then fear. He tries to cover it, so that no one will see. He begins to feel shame, for his celebrated beauty begins to fade. Lucas is afraid of what that would mean about him so he creates a shield of light over everything that is going on inside of him so that no one will see. He tries to hide what's inside, but I can feel that he is slipping. I see the first moment Lucas is too proud to show the Creator how he feels.

The Creator tries to channel his love to Lucas, but Lucas cannot receive it. His eyes are no longer on the Creator without fail. Lucas feels betrayed. The pain in his heart deepens until it is as deep as the love once was. Lucas is in agony. I feel the agony, it gets deeper with every moment that passes. With a sweeping, circular sensation, his love turns to hatred. I feel the pain, and my heart longs to ease it.

Something pulls me back to consciousness. The tune and tone of Lucas' song has changed to a brighter version of what he was humming when our meditation began. I open my eyes. He is there, in front of me. He has just revealed something to me in his song.

"I saw," I say.

"I showed you," he replies.

I reach my hand to his face, running my fingers over the surface of his cool smooth skin. My heart aches, overwhelmed with emotion. I begin to weep. Lucas embraces me. It's just too much for me to bear. I melt into him. *Why do I feel this way?* My head rests on Lucas' chest, I can hear the vibration of the words that he speaks, even this vibration sounds like music.

"I trust you Eve. I've shared something with you that no one else has known. I once had a great love. You felt only a small portion of the reality of that love. You also felt the consequence of that love when it was betrayed. I lived for the Creator; my mind had no other thought, my heart no other love, my life no other purpose. When I lost that love, my life meant nothing. Until I met you. I showed you only a glimpse, yet I am afraid that I have shared too much. I didn't mean to hurt you." He lifts my chin. I feel completely vulnerable and stripped. A rush of warm energy engulfs me, as it always does when he looks at me this way. I have no idea how he does this. It comforts me more now than ever.

Fully connected to each other, eyes linked in an intimate gaze of two unshielded beings he says to me, "That is why I teach you non attachment. My dream for you is self-reliance, for I never want you to know the depth of despair that I have felt." He strokes my hair, "Eve, with me here, things will be different for you, I promise. You shall never know heartbreak. I shall never betray you."

My heart is stretched beyond its previous capacity. Witnessing pain for the first time, feeling the ravages of it, opens a raw emotion within me: compassion.

We sit in silent communion for a long time. It got dark, I knew I should return to Adam, but I couldn't. I couldn't look into Adams eyes and be casual. I couldn't share my experience with him, he wouldn't understand. He couldn't possibly understand the depth of my emotion because he hadn't experienced the type of connection that I shared with Lucas. It would be impossible to return home and be *normal*. I had changed.

I stay with Lucas. Together we sit in thoughtless silence. After many hours I stir. Stretching a body that ached from stillness. I take a deep breath and yawn, the motion of which broke our silent reverie.

"What happened between you and the Creator, Lucas?" I ask, ready to talk again. The shock of the vision faded. I rest my head on his chest and place my hand on his heart. It didn't beat like Adam's. Lucas was silent, he seemed to contemplate whether or not he should share his story with me. I look up at his beautiful face. He looks into the distance. Silent. I give him time.

After a long moment he whispers, "I'd like to show you, but I don't think that you are strong enough. How the last vision affected you, it was too much for me to witness." He shakes his head, "I don't want to hurt you anymore than I already have."

The compassion rises in deep waves from my heart, rolling off of me like mist from the sea. "I want to know. I want to understand."

"There is a way," he says. "Something that you can do to prepare your mind, your body, and your soul - for the truth."

"Anything. I'll do it," I speak without hesitation.

He is silent.

"What can I do?" I ask.

"Eve, you must be sure, for what I'm about to suggest - you can never come back from it. You will be forever changed. This is a very serious decision, to know the truth. You will lose your innocence and know the reality of pain after tonight. I don't know if I can take away your innocence so that you may know my story."

"I want to know, Lucas. Tell me how," I plead.

He takes a breath and looks into my eyes for one long last moment. He strokes my hair and kisses my head. I can feel the regret in his touch. A tear forms at the corner of his eye. "I'll show you. I want you to know. We can be together after this night, forever."

He begins to sing a variation of the song that drew me to him, the song he was singing the day that we met. I feel my consciousness slip into another plane, a timeless dimension. Lucas stands, holding his hand out for mine. The notes of his song clear the reality around us. I feel as if I am in a dream of clarity as he pulls me to my feet.

Singing still, he leads me by the hand into the clearing in the center of the garden. The notes of his song blend seamlessly with the melody of the trees. As his notes become stronger so does that of the trees. The three are singing an eternal song of love, longing and loss. The notes haunt every cell in my body. He leads me to The Tree of the Knowledge of Good and Evil. His notes hit a high and the fruit, which is liquid light encased in crystal cubes of ice begin to reverberate against one another. I feel a vague fear somewhere in the back of my mind, but it is only a shadow in the light of my trust in Lucas; existing only as an afterthought to a question that was never asked: *should I trust him?*

The heat of The Tree of Life behind me burns my back. Its fruit, like the sun, screams for me to stop. The heat surges strongly, as if an attempt to melt the crystal cubes before I can touch them. The heat burns my back, but my mind is on the mysterious tree in front of me. All of my questions, all of the puzzles in my mind, every wondering that I have had about the trees, Lucas, the Creator, and my own life will soon be answered. Lucas leads my hand into the cold. My finger touches the tip of a cube. An intense power originating from the cube moves through my fingertip, overwhelming my body. My head feels light, like I am about to faint, yet something in the notes of Lucas' song propels my hand forward. The mystery in his voice, the clarity of his notes, the pain, the loss, the love all intermingled; touching every nerve in my body.

I pluck one of the cubes from the tree. It falls from the branch with surprising ease. I can feel the ice melt, the moisture dissipates immediately. My hand freezes all the way to the bone; cool, electric waves surge through my hand into my entire body in short erratic pulses. I move the ice to my lips. The moment the cube touches my lips - it melts, and my entire body is enraptured as the first molecules of light are absorbed into my flesh. Everything stopped.

Time stops. The garden is still.

Birds stop, mid-flight, suspended in the air.

I fall back. Lucas catches me, holds me in his arms.

The Universe opens up to me.

Simultaneously two things happen. First the sensations in my body explode. It is orgasmic and all consuming. I can feel the light, first absorbed in my mouth spread and circulate into every cell in my body. The second thing that happens is a tangible expansion of my mind. I feel it being pulled in all directions at once, enlightening my consciousness to a vast awareness and knowledge. Into my brain a cold and intense laser beams from the Universe through the top of my head, recalibrating, stretching and expanding the physical mass inside, the sound of which is deafening.

As suddenly as it began, all motion inside of me stops.

My heart stops.

My mind stops.

My breath stops.

All is silent.

The transformation is complete.

Chapter 11

The first thing that I notice is the dueling whisper of universal secrets. The trees in the clearing are speaking. My hearing now more acute, I can hear the mystical conversation clearly. I had once mistaken their conversation for music. One speaks of the world as it could have been; the other speaks of the world as it is now. Possibility and Reality.

I turn my eyes to Lucas and see him, as if for the first time. His beauty is awe-inspiring. There is nothing like him in all of creation. My vision is clear and able to perceive the smallest and most imperceptible details of his skin. What formerly looked like an iridescent luminosity is now seen to be a tiny, complex, and ancient script etched onto the planes of his flesh. His light shines from within through the etchings, casting a luminescent glow, highlighting and giving life to each word. His eyes, the eyes that drew me before, are now impossible to look away from. Deep, deeper than deep, I see into eternity. His hair a crown of black silk, now loose, falls in waves around his shoulders.

We gaze at each other in knowing silence. I am completely present with him. Equal. All of eternity surrounds us like a timeless black cloak.

"It is time," Lucas says. As he speaks, I can see the energy of his spoken words wisp on his breath, dance with the molecules in the air between us, changing each one as it passes, and finally merge into my energy field where it is absorbed into my being. Astounded, I realize that the spoken word is an energy transmission. Speaking is no longer just speaking. It is a living, creative force. I watch the space between us with acute fascination. Lucas sees my interest in the process and explains, "There is water in the air molecules. Do you remember, Eve? The first day we met by the lake, I told you there is magic in the water. Now that you have tasted the truth of The Tree of Knowledge you can see. Water is a conductor of energy. The intention, or the energy, of my words is transmitted, conducted through the water in the air and then absorbed into your body, which is also made mostly of water. This Earth too," he motions around us, "is also primarily this substance. You, the air, the Earth, all comprised of this great conductor. It is what connects you; this was all created as a perfect circuitry so that life and energy pass seamlessly from one thing to the next. There is much to explain, and all will be revealed to you." He bows his head to look into my eyes, "The time has come, the reason we are here." He steps closer to me, a breath away. Taking my hand he places it on the cool flesh of his cheek. "I want you to read my story. For once you know my story, you will understand everything."

Looking at the mystical script on his face, I run my fingers along the edge of his hairline. I see only the name of God, written over and over, interlinking in beautiful detail. My fingers move to the next line, again God's name. Line after line I only see the name of God.

"Eve", Lucas calls my attention to his eyes. He stands before me in all of his glory. "To understand my story you must not read only the surface letters of the text, to know the true meaning you must experience them. Do not use your mind. Touch the first word, now close your eyes. Breathe, feel your body, feel the space around your body. Now feel your fingertips, feel the surface of my skin, my story." His words lull me deeper into the experience. "Now, feel the meaning of the word beneath your fingers."

With a spark, a crackle of lightning, I am transported to another time. A time before time. Before the Earth was created. I stand there, feeling the first word in the story of Lucas' life.

It was God. In that moment I knew God.

I remain in that presence of divine peace, in the presence of God, and I want for nothing. There is nothing but that presence.

Lucas takes my hand, gently removing it from the text. Still in the divine energy of the Creator I open my eyes. Love and contentment fill my being, causing a tear to run down my cheek. Lucas allows my hand to fall to my side. My body feels light, almost formless. I stand with no effort at all.

"The entirety of my experience is here, etched onto my skin. To know my story you must read all of it," Lucas says, an open vulnerability in his face. "Every thought, every word, every experience is recorded here. It is the story of my life."

Lucas gingerly opens his robe, revealing his chest. The holy text continues down the surface of his neck, chest and abdomen. His skin, a silver pale white, looks like marble in the moonlight, the ancient engravings of his life written in light. He wears a sheer white sarong tied at the waist. Lucas allows the robe to fall from his shoulders; it slips to the ground with a whisper.

"Let us sit, Eve." He leads me to the ground. We sit in lotus posture, our knees touching. Lucas' hair falls behind his shoulders in lacquered waves. He is a luminous angel. He holds his hand out for mine and I place my palm in his. Leading my hand to his forehead, we again begin at the beginning of his story - transported into the experiences of his life, and I experience every moment as he had.

Chapter 12
Heaven

There is harmony in and all around me. Billows of intricately laced fog layer the floor. Lavender at the base, rising to a gentle pink, folds of the lightest blues and golds tone their way throughout, weaving softly. The sky above is the most beautiful shade of yellow that I have ever seen, it is both soft and vibrant in its luxurious subtlety. It is diffused, like sunshine through honey. I stand in Lucas' memory, looking around with acute fascination. Everything is light. Everything has form but it is not like it is on Earth. Form on Earth is dense. Here, forms are fluid and shift according to thought. Each being holds its form consciously and everything moves in a continuous shift of various stages of bloom. There are no clear lines. Every line is soft and blows in an unseen wind, shifting as lines in the sand.

Being an angel, you can be anything. The only limit is your imagination and courage in declaring it so. Being an angel is an invitation to draw from the limitless attributes of the Creator and become what you dare imagine yourself to be. An angel chooses its form based upon the attribute of the Creator that it most desires to celebrate. There are some angels who yield mighty swords of fire, drawing fiercely upon the Lord's bravery and might. Others, gentle as doves wings, express the eternal peace of the Creator. There are the wise ones, carefully keeping record of every event within the kingdom. Others still who laugh and dance in an eternal expression of the Creator's playfulness. Then there is Lucas. Beautiful, breathtaking Lucas.

Here, Lucas goes by another name, a name the Creator chose for this vessel of divine light. He was given the name Lucifer, The Bearer of Light. Lucifer's name has many meanings, each one describing an aspect. He is also called The Son of the Morning, the Morning Star, Day Star, and The Light Bringer.

Though he is an angel, expressing that which is already existent within the Creator, there is something remarkable about him. He expresses not just one or two of the attributes of the Creator, but many. Looking at his heavenly form I can see the nobility, the creativity, and his natural ability to channel large volumes of the light of God, sharing it with his mere presence. But most interestingly of all is his ability to direct that light, at will, with his voice. His song echoes hauntingly throughout the heavens. His voice cuts through the air like forked, silver lassoes with a clear and intense love. This music is ceaseless. When he is with the Creator, he sings directly to the Creator of his greatness, his divine beauty and love. When he is not in the direct presence of the Creator, Lucifer's song laments the time until he is again.

Lucifer beams divine light, channeling everything that is within him back to the Creator through his devotion. No other angel's beauty can compare to Lucifer's; as his beauty is in direct relation to his devotion to the Lord. *That is what true beauty is; devotion to the Creator.*

Nothing pleases the Lord more than Lucifer's song. The Lord loves Lucifer and keeps him by his side whenever possible. The existence of a heavenly family comes into my knowing. The Lord of heavens has a wife, a great comforter, known as the Heavenly Spirit. He also has a Son, Jesus. The three make the one, and the one make the trinity. They are all aspects of the one great power.

Lucifer and Jesus are dear friends. Together they perform great works. Lucifer with his voice and Jesus with his hands. Jesus creates and plays instruments and Lucifer adds his voice to the creation. The two can transform the form of any being with a single note. They have great fun with this art - often changing female angels into male, red haired angels into raven, tall into short, thin into voluptuous. Each creation is more divine and beautiful then the last. With this music the energy of the Lord is channeled further into each of the beings of heaven. All of the angels adore them, and delight in their play. The trinity delights in Lucifer and Lucifer delights in the trinity. They celebrate and enjoy the collaboration.

Crisp, cool tones of a flute dance through the air. Lucifer and Jesus lean casually against the external wall of a building on a painted street corner in the main square, looking suspiciously like they are up to no good. Foot traffic flows in waves. Jesus leans in and whispers something in Lucifer's ear. Lucifer laughs, nodding head as he winks. Jesus brings a flute to his lips to test his instrument. He blows one clear, crisp note into the air.

Jesus is beautiful in a very different way than Lucas. He is the model of the masculine ideal, with the physique of a working man.

Broad shoulders, strong arms and large hands. His presence is both welcoming and protective. Arms that keep you in their strength. Warm blankets and bear hugs. He is clothed in a garment of lush burgundy wine. Warm auburn eyes flecked with shimmers of gold, framed by a prominent brow. His nose is uniquely long and noble. Brown hair shines both from health and the refraction from his golden crown of light. His beard grows with perfectly squared edges along his jaw. He is unchanging. Solid. Stable. He holds the space around him in the dense, grounded reality of truth. In his presence there are no questions, only answers. He is unique in this way as here in heaven things shift with thought, continually blooming and changing. He is the mountain. Unmoving. Strong. Wise.

He blows into his instrument again, stronger this time, holding the note in an unwavering stream of consciousness. A raven haired female angel who walks along the street is instantly transforms into a tall male with flaxen hair of gold.

"Lucifer!" The angel looks at the two in warning.

Lucifer and Jesus laugh. Shaking his head, Lucifer holds his hands up to convey his innocence, "It wasn't me!"

The angel shakes its head, raven hair flies, replacing the gold. Female replaces male. She is back to her original form. She looks at the two in indignant warning. Lucifer points to Jesus. When she looks at Jesus, her expression softens and she shakes her head,

"You two up to mischief again?"

"Of course," Lucifer replies, with a smile.

"I'll leave you two to it then. Just try to stay out of trouble will you?" she smiles, continuing her stride.

"Us? Trouble? Never." Lucifer winks.

She smiles, blushing at his attention.

"Urieon?" Lucifer asks.

She turns around and meets his eyes, "Yes?"

"*God bless you*," as the blessing passes Lucifer's lips, swirls of light twist around the raven haired angel, pulling her spine straight, lengthening her neck. A brand of light, one of the many names of God, the next level in the angel's progression of intimacy with the Creator, is etched upon her forehead, advancing her consciousness to the next level of being.

A tear falls down her cheek. "Thank you," she whispers.

This is why Lucifer is called *The Light Bringer*.

"You are welcome, Urieon. Now go, and let your light shine in the world."

Jesus looks at Lucifer in surprise. "You've become more powerful, Lucifer."

"It is not my power, but that of my Father," Lucifer's tone fills with love.

"Your power lies in devotion," Jesus replies, nodding his head astutely.

How can I not be filled with devotion? Devotion is all I could possibly know, knowing the trinity as I do. Your grace is unending. Each time I expand my mind to its farthest reaches, there it remains. It knows no boundaries. It is infinite. That is what I love the most about you, no matter how far I challenge myself, how far I expand; you are there, one step ahead of me encouraging me to be more. I do not deserve such love," Lucifer says. He looks up and spies something that makes his eyes fill with the light of enthusiasm. "Jesus, look who's coming..."

The Heavenly Spirit, the female aspect of God walks toward them. She is divine. Her olive skin, wise almond eyes and gently angled face is the portrait of perfection. Lucifer has never seen anything more beautiful than his wise Mother. She wears silver garments of silk that shift elegantly over her generous figure as she walks. The fine silk rolls like storm clouds over her round, voluptuous belly, pregnant with life. She seems to float, each step perfectly balanced, perfectly poised, gliding through the space as if she were dancing to a symphony of strings. She smiles at Lucifer in recognition. He looks at her with the fascination of a pupil enraptured in the presence of his favorite teacher. Lucifer bows his head, holding it in quiet reverence.

Raising his eyes, Lucifer whispers to Jesus, "Watch this."

Lucifer opens his mouth and hits the purest, most honest note that the heavens has ever heard. Shimmers surround the Heavenly Mother's face in twinkles of light. At once her face is transformed, now an exact replica of the Heavenly Father's. Her fingers raise to feel its contours. At once she laughs, her merriment fills the air. "Lucifer!"

Lucifer looks at Jesus, who is laughing, "Why does everyone blame me?"

Jesus socks Lucifer's shoulder. "Maybe it's because of your reputation... besides it *was* you."

"*This time,*" Lucifer interjects.

"Don't worry Mother, I'll get him back for you." Jesus calls. He raises the flute to his lips and with one breath Lucifer's wings of platinum ignite into flames. Jesus laughs. Lucifer looks back at his wings and howls,

"Jesus! No!"

The Heavenly Mother waves her hand to quell the fire. Her face returns to its original form. Lucifer looks at his wings in disbelief. The heat from the fire has melted each individual feather of platinum into one large mass. "Jesus!" Lucifer accuses, shock twists his features.

"Don't worry Lucifer, I'll turn them back." Jesus raises his flute and in a blink Lucifer's wings are restored.

Lucifer sighs in frustration, "They are not the same."

"They look the same to me," Jesus appraises.

"They aren't. Jesus, why would you do that?"

"I'm sorry, Lucifer," Jesus apologizes. "We change things all of the time. On you, on me, on everyone around us. I didn't think you'd mind."

"I had a feather of platinum for every prayer that I have ever made to the Creator, every blessing that I have given. Those were not just any charms; they were my *record of devotion*. They meant something to me. These," Lucifer points to the restored wings behind him, "these are counterfeit. Now I will have to start over again."

"Lucifer, I am sorry," Jesus says, earnestly.

The Heavenly Mother puts one hand on Lucifer's shoulder and smiles with a quiet compassion, "It was an honest mistake. Jesus did nothing more than what you yourself have done countless times to others."

"But they meant something to me," Lucifer protests.

"Do not be attached to sentimental tokens Lucifer. It's a good thing that this happened, so that you could see that your wings were a source of attachment and pride. Consider this a lesson learned."

For the first time Lucifer is frustrated with the trinity. He doesn't understand the strong emotions that stir within him. Defensively, he tries to explain, "It is not my wings that I was attached to, but what they meant. Each tier was a reminder of my love for you, a signature of where I was and what I was doing when they were created. They were my record, my keepsake, my memory; the first of which was my very moment of my creation. I have acquired them over an eternity, now, they are gone. These may look the same, but they are not."

"It's your actual love for us, not the representation of your love, that is beautiful, Lucifer. They are gone. You need to accept that and move forward. What would you like to do? Keep these or start over?" She looks at him with a firm compassion.

Lucifer considers. He doesn't want a counterfeit, a fake, for every time he looks at them he will be reminded of the empty promise that each one held, but he is afraid that the other angels will think that he had done something wrong to lose his wings. He was admittedly embarrassed to be without them, ashamed at the assumptions that others might make. He is torn. "Is there something that the Creator can do?" he asks.

"We can ask Him," The Heavenly Mother offers.

Jesus offers his hand to Lucifer to help him stand, "Sorry, brother. If I had known," he shakes his head, genuinely disturbed.

Lucifer sighs, accepting the gesture. "It's alright. You couldn't have known. I may have over reacted. I'm just in shock."

"All hope is not lost though. I will ask the Father if he will access the moment of ignition and retrieve them," Jesus offers.

"Thank you, Jesus," Lucifer exhales deeply.

Jesus slaps him on the back, "We'll call for you soon, hopefully with good news."

****

"I have good news, and I have bad news. Which do you want first?"

Lucifer looks at Jesus with dread, knowing what is coming. "He can't restore my original wings?"

Jesus looks down, "No. For many reasons. The most important of all being that He thinks that this will be a growth experience for you."

Lucifer's heart sinks. There was no arguing with the Creator, he is the final word. "What's the good news?"

Jesus smiles, "I want to make it up to you. I've already consulted within the trinity and we want you to help us architect plans for a world we are creating. Would you like that?"

Lucifer's face brightens as he comprehends the importance of this unique offer. He almost can't believe that the trinity would ask his help for such a task. He is elated, "Yes! Of course. It would be my honor."

Jesus embraces Lucifer heartily, "I'm glad! We'll start right away. First order of business, have you decided if you want to keep the replacement wings or not?"

Lucifer considers his options again, "I would not."

"Are you sure? Nobody will know."

"I will."

Jesus smiles, "I'm sure that you'll have new ones, *twice as large*, in no time at all." He waves his hand and the counterfeit wings disappear. Getting right to business, Jesus sits at a table in Lucifer's sparse quarters. Lucifer likes to keep his possessions few. He lives very simply. Sleeping quarters, sitting area, and a place to eat is all that he requires. Clean lines and few objects, none of the ornate gold gilding that is so popular in the heavens.

Jesus explains the task at hand, "We want to create eight planets, with eight dimensions. Each planet will inhabit beings at different levels of consciousness, each progressing toward the kingdom of heaven. Do you have something we can record this on?" Jesus looks to Lucifer expectantly.

"Of course." Lucifer places a tablet and writing utensil on the table.

Picking up the tools and beginning to draw, Jesus continues, "Each planet will be primarily made of individual and unique elements, such as: Fire, Air, Wind, Metal, Water, Ether, Sediment and Gas. Each planet will bear one of the names of God, highlighting the aspect of Him that world will possess. We will begin with the third planet; this is the one that we would like your input on."

"Why start with the third? Why not the first?"

"Three is the number of the trinity."

Lucifer nods his head, "Where will these planets be located?"

"They will neighbor the kingdom of heaven, in subsequent order to the level of consciousness of the planet."

"How will they be positioned?"

"In a straight line, but they will rotate around the kingdom of heaven."

"Can you elaborate?" Lucifer questions.

"The planets will revolve around the kingdom. The light of the kingdom will warm and nurture the planets. All life will be dependent upon the energy of God. Each planet will rotate on its own axis so that all sides of the sphere will receive the equal attention of the Creator."

"What happens to the side of the planet when it is turned away from the kingdom?"

Jesus smiles wryly, "It will be dark."

Lucifer laughs. "Yes, but without direct contact with the light of God how will life be sustained on the dark side of the planet?"

Jesus considers Lucifer's question, "We could build in an energy solar cell in each creation so that it can last through the night. Or life could perish at night and begin again each day, but that would mean that each of the beings would have to evolve very quickly to progress.

"What is the element of the planet we are working on?" Lucifer asks, reaching into his imagination.

"Water," Jesus says.

Inspired with an idea, Lucifer begins to speak, thinking out loud, "To ensure that the light of God will spread fluidly throughout the planet we could make water a conductor of energy. If we make this element the basic foundation of life on the planet, the flora and fauna, the air and the atmosphere would literally circuit the energy of God from one thing to the next, without interruption, regardless if the portion of the planet is facing the kingdom or not. All things could communicate the presence of God without doing so consciously."

Jesus' eyes brighten. "That would also help the beings on the planet evolve collectively. Brilliant Lucifer!"

"What about form, dense or fluid?" Lucifer asks.

"Both," Jesus replies. "Fluid, with changeable dense forms. There will be oceans and animals, masses of land, great mountains and life. No detail or extravagance will be left out. We should push our imaginations to the limit on this one. We should also make this planet self renewing and self-supporting."

"How long do we have?" Lucifer begins to pace.

"I'd like to present the rough plans to Him tonight."

"We'd better get to work." Lucifer claps his hands together, rubbing his palms. He has never known the joy of creating such intricacies before and he finds the whole process intoxicating. He realizes that he, in this honorable position, will have the chance to experience what it was like to be God, to create. He has a new appreciation toward and for the trinity for bestowing upon him this great honor.

Chapter 13

Lucifer paces back and forth, tidying his few possessions nervously. He awaits word from Jesus detailing the Creator's response to their original draft for the planet Earth. His heart jumps when he hears a knock at the door. When he swings the door open he is greeted with Jesus' congratulatory smile.

"He loves it," Jesus says.

"Yeah?" Lucifer beams.

"Yeah. He will start the creation process first thing tomorrow." Jesus steps past Lucifer, and sits on the mat in the common area.

"That soon?" The beat of Lucifer's heart doubles, he follows Jesus inside, closing the door behind him.

"He loves it and wants to start straight away," Jesus leans back, extending his legs on the carpet casually.

Lucifer exhales and sits next to Jesus. He hadn't realized that he had been holding his breath. The enormity of the project he has contributed to washes over him… he had helped God create a planet. The entire process was intoxicating; the ownership of his contribution is almost too large for his vessel to house. He can feel his consciousness expand yet again.

"How do you feel?" Jesus asks, eyes him with curiosity.

"Overwhelmed. Happy."

"There is more."

Lucifer looks at Jesus, a look of amazement paints his features, "More?"

"Yes," Jesus says.

The smile Jesus flashed sent shivers down Lucifer's spine. He can tell that whatever news Jesus has to share is going to be huge. "What is it?!"

Jesus looks deeply into Lucifer's eyes, "The Father wants you to be the light bearer for this planet, the morning star, to serve as the herald of the dawn. It would be you that would announce the arrival of the Father's presence each morning."

"Me?" Lucifer's voice caught in his throat.

"Yes," Jesus laughs.

Lucifer jumps to his feet, pulling Jesus with him. He wraps his arms around Jesus with all of his might, lifting him in the air with a ferocious bear hug, spinning him around the room. This was quite a feat, as Jesus is the only dense, solid being in heaven. *It was like a feather lifting a mountain.* Lucifer doesn't notice the weight.

"Are we to assume your answer is 'yes'?" Jesus laughs heartily.

"Yes! A thousand times, yes!" Lucifer calls, his voice carries through the heavens.

"Great Lucifer! We have many plans for you, many more projects that we want your help on. There are seven other planets in this solar system that we will develop, just as the Earth.

"It would be my honor. Thank you for this opportunity." Lucifer bows, his eyes fill with the tears of gratitude.

****

The first day of the great construction God created the Heavens, placing the kingdom of heaven within a sphere of light. Then came the planets, spread through the space surrounding the heavens. When God focused his attention on the Earth, he created the oceans and the fish of the sea. From the sea rose great masses of land, vegetation, and animals to inhabit the land. On the sixth day God created Adam, the human that was to live upon the Earth. Adam was the Creator's own special project. The details of which were disclosed to no one. He also created a tree that would act as God's individuated presence in the garden. He called it The Tree of Life and located it in the center of the paradise. This tree bore fruit that were replicas of the kingdom of heaven, of the sun. He created it so that The Father and Adam could communicate through this tree. On the seventh day, God rested.

*****

A great celebration had erupted in the kingdom of heaven, the likes of which had never been seen before. In celebration, all of the angels in heaven danced in golden the streets. Jesus and Lucifer sang and played the most joyous of music. It was a celebration larger than that the heavens have ever seen before. All of the beings in heaven gathered to celebrate the Creator for his miraculous ability to channel enough energy to create such a vast and perfect universe

"Lucifer! What happened to your wings?" Youvanah asks as she makes her way through the crowd to stand by Lucifer. She cocks her head of cornsilk curls inquisitively. Youvanah is one of Lucifer's few friends in the heavens. Not that he isn't celebrated by many, but Lucifer is a bit of a loner. He spends most of his time in communion with the trinity. But Youvanah was different, her bright blue eyes inspired Lucifer with their kindness. She had a gentle smile that followed him wherever he went. Youvanah treated Lucifer as her mentor, which endeared her to him. He musses her curls, answering her question with a smile,

"Jesus accidentally burst them into flames."

"Accidentally?" She raises an eyebrow.

Lucifer laughs, "Yeah, you know how he can be. We were messing around and it went a little too far."

She hesitates, eyeing the change. "You look different, but good. It's a good look for you."

"Really?" Lucifer is surprised by her answer. An angel's wings were their pride and joy. Without them he felt naked.

"Just you watch, within a few days half the angels here will have sheared their wings, too." Her eyes flash with amusement, "If it's possible you are shining brighter than usual. Wings, or no wings."

Lucifer nods his head. There is no question in his mind as to why. Through his contribution to the Creator's process of creation his consciousness has elevated to new heights. He literally felt his spirit grow bigger and brighter, making him more feel more confident, more capable. The flurry of activity around them catches their attention; a whisper had passed through the crowd.

"What's going on?" Lucifer asked his protégé.

She looks at him, eyes wide with excitement, and whispers, "The Creator is here. He is going to make an announcement."

"An announcement? Really?" Lucifer had not heard about this from the trinity. He's as surprised as the rest of the crowd. The Heavenly Spirit enters the stage from the left; the luxurious yellow sky frames her olive skin and dark upswept hair. On the stage there are three thrones made from the deepest velvet of blue. She sits on the throne furthest to the left, sinking with a soft purpose. She is still, poised; a peaceful smile plays on her lips. Jesus follows; his robes of wine flow fluidly as he walks, the golden rope tied at his waist sways like temple bells. Sinking onto the chair, he takes a moment to look over the crowd; smiling and nodding each time he makes eye contact with the collecting crowd of angels.

A hush blows through the crowd when a single harpsichord begins to play, its notes meant to announce the arrival of the Creator. Both Jesus and the Heavenly Spirit rise. A massive form of light ascends the stage. There are no distinctive qualities to the Creator's form. He just is light. A bright light, a peaceful fire, lightning, pure energy. In a whisper all angels fall to their knees, resting their foreheads on the ground. A silent moment passes as all of the beings in heaven absorb the light of the Creator. This is quite a unique happening, the Creator making a public address.

With each second that passes, Lucifer's excitement grows. He wonders what the Creator will announce. Perhaps He will announce His unprecedented decision to allow Lucifer to help draft the plans for the Earth? Perhaps it will be His decision to appoint Lucifer as the Morning Star for this planet? Perhaps he will make a public request for Lucifer to help him rule this planet? It made sense, Lucifer will be there anyway, heralding the light of the Creator each moment of each day. Keeping an eye on things would for the Creator made complete sense. And doing so would sort of feel like he had a kingdom of his own. Perhaps the Lord would use this opportunity as a test. Lucifer's imagination soars with the possibilities, each one fueling his elation further.

"Rise," The Creator's voice fills each being's heart.

Lucifer loves to hear the Creator speak. The Creator is pure presence and speaks only on the rarest of occasions; when he does, it is a gift beyond all understanding… because it is the Creator's *actual* voice. It's almost too much energy for Lucifer to bear. It is amazing, the power His voice yields. It is the power of His voice with which He creates. The creation of the Universe started with a single word. That is why it is a rarity to hear the voice of the Creator, as the power that it yields is something that the Creator uses sparingly. In most instances His angel Gabriel conveys the Creator's message, diluting the energy of the message enough to be consumable by the masses. Sometimes it is the Heavenly Spirit or Jesus who dictates the Lord's message, but rarely the Lord Himself. That is why this is such a momentous occasion.

"A new Universe has been created," As the Creator speaks, the energy from his words creates a three dimensional picture in front of him, expressing his words in pictures. There is no need to imagine what he is talking about; the image clearly demonstrates what he is trying to convey.

"I have finished creating life on the third planet from the kingdom of heaven," He continues. "This planet is called Earth. This new planet will be ruled by a creature called *Man*. I have created man in my image, he is an extension of me, and therefore you shall treat man as you would treat me. Adam has been created to rule the Earth, he is my son."

Lucifer's mouth drops open. His entire body pricks with shock. He checks the three-dimensional picture to see if he heard correctly. He did. The form of the man's chest and forehead are filled with the same light that the Creator is. Pure light, peaceful fire, lightning and energy. Lucifer is taken aback, unable believe how foolish he had been to think for a moment that the Creator would ask *him* to rule the Earth. Pangs of jealousy arise in his chest. This is an unfamiliar emotion to Lucifer. He takes a deep breath, trying to quiet his mind, trying to bring himself into the present moment - to hear the rest of what the Creator has to say, but his mind returns to this creature called man. Indignant anger rises like a quiet flame within him. Each time he quenches the flame, it rises up again, devouring him from within. Lucifer's attention is not on the Creator at all, but rather within his own mind, trying desperately to manage this uprising of hate.

He knew that he couldn't walk out of the auditorium, but he wished he could. He needed to be alone. This urge surprises him; he has never *not* wanted to be in the presence of the Creator before. He imagines the hushed questions pass through the crowd if he were to walk out while the Lord was speaking. He doesn't want to cause a scene, so he forces himself to stay.

"...and that brings me to Lucifer."

The sound of God speaking his name pulls Lucifer from the deep recesses of his mind.

"Lucifer has been selected to be the Light Bringer for this planet, the Son of the Morning. It is Lucifer who will announce my Presence on the Earth each day. Lucifer, please come to the stage."

Thousands of angel's faces turn to look at him. He bows, graciously, and makes his way to the stage, stopping to smile and greet each angel that congratulates him along the way. Once on stage Lucifer bows to the trinity and turns to face the crowd. Cheers erupt. Heady waves of excitement wash over him as he accepts the jubilant admiration from the crowd.

****

The Father descends the stage. The even has ended. Lucifer turns to Jesus and smiles weakly. Looking genuinely confused Jesus asks,

"Lucifer, what is it? Why the forlorn expression?"

Lucifer hesitates, he doesn't want to seem ungrateful, but he is disturbed. He exhales and explains, "I don't know. I feel confused… and strange."

Jesus beckons the Heavenly Mother to join them. At once she comes, placing a tender palm on Lucifer's shoulder, "What is it?"

Lucifer turns to her, speaks in a quiet voice, "I don't know. I just feel, *sad*."

"Sad?" She smiles, "Oh, Son of the Morning, there is nothing to be sad about on this great day. What's bothering you?"

Lucifer hesitates, he doesn't want to seem ungrateful. But he also feels compelled to be honest. "Jesus and I have designed this world, shouldn't it be our honor to rule it?"

She smiles knowingly, "You feel some ownership because you helped with the conception of the planet and now you want to express that ownership fully? That is a natural reaction, Lucifer, but we want you here, with us. We love you. You bring more joy to the trinity than any other being in creation. We want you to stay with us, here in heaven, to help with the conception of the other planets. Does this not satisfy you?"

"I know it should, but I *want* the responsibility of ruling a planet. I think that I am ready," Lucifer explains.

"Only the Creator can rule a planet, Lucifer. That is the way that it has always been," she replies.

"But what about Adam? He's not the Creator."

"He is an aspect of the Creator."

"But so am I," Lucifer tried to temper the whine in his voice. He hated that he was acting so immature, but he couldn't help himself. What he said was true.

The Heavenly Mother looks at him with compassion, "You are… but you must understand that Man is different. He was created to fulfill this role. We all have our duty. His duty is there. Your duty is here with us."

Lucifer couldn't comprehend why this honor was being passed to another. He did not understand, yet he respected the wisdom of the trinity's choices. He nods once, "If it is your wish, I will stay."

She smiles, "That is our wish. Just wait, my dear. You will understand one day."

"Thank you for taking the time to hear me," he says, bowing his head.

"Of course, my love." She leans forward to kiss Lucifer's forehead, filling his mind with light. He has no more questions or concerns. His mind is numbingly contented from the love she blows into him.

*****

As time passed in the heavens, the Father spent more and more time gazing upon the garden through The Tree of Life. It seemed to Lucifer that the Father was showing more love toward Adam than he showed him. His heart became heavy. The harmony between Lucifer and the trinity began to break down, and for the first time in his existence, Lucifer felt alone.

Lucifer continued to sing, but his song had become more of a haunted lament than a celebration of light. Lucifer's songs haunted the hearts of all in the heavens, which stirred a division amongst its inhabitants. The anguish of his notes swayed many of the heavenly hearts into feel compassion for him. While others, due to the pain that Lucifer's agonized notes evoked in their hearts, found it easier to avoid him. Lucifer didn't care that he had become an outcast in their society, for he had to express what was in his heart. He had been passed over, abandoned, and wounded. With this a new name for Lucifer was born: *Son of Mourning.*

The Father's heart broke, just as did Lucifer's. He couldn't take another moment of Lucifer's pain. Determined, the Lord calls him to court, to find a solution for Lucifer, no matter what it took.

Lucifer responds to God's call. He walks in, face drawn. His light has dimmed so much, he is a shadow of his former self. With His reaching heart, the Lord looks at Lucifer and wonders: *Was this the Angel that had once been the brightest in all of the heavens?* The fall was a hard one to watch.

"Lucifer, this has gone too far," The Lord speaks in light. "Please, take my hand once more and return into harmony with the trinity. I know your heart, you don't want to spend your life suffering. You must accept reality, and be grateful for the position that you hold. I have chosen for Adam to rule the Earth, and for you to help me create new planets."

"But Father, I feel like you have deemed me not worthy to rule a land of my own. I wouldn't ask if I didn't think that I was ready."

"You truly feel that you are ready?" the Lord asked.

"I do," he answered.

"What then, do you propose that I do?"

"Give the Earth to me."

"What right do you have to rule the Earth, Lucifer? Has man shown himself unworthy? You suggest that you are responsible enough to rule a planet with creatures of free will, yet when you were disappointed here in the heavens you can hardly function. What happens when you are under duress with the inhabitants of the Earth, what should you do then? It takes great patience, fortitude, and wisdom to be a king."

Lucifer's sorrow elevates to rage, "You think man has proven himself more than me? I have given you everything, pledged my every fiber to you... and in return you have given everything to Man - who has given you nothing. It's not fair. What makes him more worthy than *me*?"

"I created man," the Lord replied. "You were not privy to the details of my creation. How can you say that you know what man is capable of when you have not even spent a moment with him, yourself? You know nothing, Lucifer."

****

With that, my vision ended. Lucas has taken my hand from his abdomen, thus ending the tour through his memories. I see Lucas with new eyes, seeing his beautiful complexity.

"It was us," I said. "We are the reason that you're no longer with the beloved. Oh, Lucas, how could this happen?"

Lucas pulls his robe over his shoulders, "I don't know, Eve." Tears stream down his face as he reaches for me. Silently, mournfully, we hold each other. He takes my chin in his hand, raising my face to look into his eyes, "That is why I am here, to prevent you from undergoing the same fate. You are the beloved of the Creator now, but the day may come that He creates something he loves more, something he chooses over you. There are seven other planets. What is to stop Him from abandoning you once he has created something that he loves more? I couldn't bear it if I had to watch you go through the same thing that I did. I love you, my Eve. I was there the night Adam asked for a companion. My final act in the heavens was to help the Lord conceive you. I helped create you, not with my power, no, I don't have the power to create, but I did help conceive you. Through that process, I developed a deep love for you. Then I met you, and you are even more delightful than I could have imagined. I am here with you now. I have left the heavens to be with you. I will never leave you." He raises my hand to his cheek, letting hit linger upon its cool flesh.

"I love you too, Lucas. What are we going to do?" I ask.

Chapter 14
Present Day

I step over the threshold of Lucas' office; the bright light from the tinted windows casts a silver haze about the room. Lucas stands by the window with his back toward me and I recall with exacting detail the first moment that I saw him in the garden, when I mistook him for the Creator, calling out to him in wonder. This human form that he possessed now was very different, still handsome, but not nearly as commanding as he once was. When he turns I see that the wounds on his face from my fiery outpouring of rage have healed. Our gaze meets, waiting for the other to break the silence. But neither of us does. The man that stands before me was my most trusted friend, and my worst enemy. He had betrayed me, disappearing from my life before I had a chance to process the implications of the temptation that he beguiled me into giving into. I have waited eons to confront him, because he was too cowardly to show his face… before now.

"I'm here. Speak," my voice sounds cold in my ears.

"Thank you for coming."

"I had no choice. You made sure of that."

"I am sorry, but there was no other way."

"Speak." A morbid curiosity fills my mind. I am curious to hear what he has to say. How will he open this conversation? Multiple emotions cross his face. He shifts his body awkwardly. *He is uncomfortable. Good.* I feel a small indignant smile pass my lips.

He searches my eyes and his face falls. I can feel what he sees there and don't try to hide it. Pain. Exhaustion. Anger.

"I've come back to you to tell you that I was wrong," he says, taking a step toward me.

I do not back away, "Continue."

A look of surprise crosses his features. He begins to speak, afraid that this opportunity will soon pass, "I was wrong. This whole place," he motions around us, "You, me, everything, has not turned out as I expected. Nothing is good anymore. Humanity is a mess, the Earth is falling apart, and you," his eyes fill with tears, "You look so tired." He eyes me tenderly. "I can feel the exhaustion in your soul. I have felt you every day; we are bound together. Every moment in your lives I have witnessed through this bond. It has come to a point where I cannot stand by and watch you digress any deeper into your anguish. The very thing that I was trying to protect you from I created in your life. I am sorry, Eve. I want to restore myself in your eyes. I want to restore the Earth as paradise… for you. I want you to be happy again. That's why I have come back, in human form, founding this company, because I think that we can do it, but I need you. I need to know that if I can restore harmony on the Earth, that you will love me once again," he finishes, completely open.

That was unexpected. I laugh, the shock of his admission, ebbs my anger. "You've come back – on a quest to restore the Earth - so that I will *date* you?" He has some nerve.

"I've changed, and I just want the opportunity for forgiveness. What comes after that, whatever it may be, I will accept. I no longer want to be a monster, Eve: in your eyes nor in the eyes of anyone else. I know that it has been bad for you, and I don't discount that, but consider for a moment how it has been for me. *I have been hated. Despised since the beginning. I just want to experience love again.* You are the only one that matters to me, so it's with you that I ask for the chance for redemption."

I am quiet. I almost can't believe what I am hearing.

"What are you thinking?" Lucas asks.

"I'm thinking about how much I hate you." I am surprised how calm I am. Had I been reunited with Lucas in any other lifetime I would have tried, futile as it would have been, to kill him. Now, I am just numb. By some miracle, I can look at him with neutral eyes because I'm too tired. The fight inside of me had finally been exhausted. In fact, I feel like I'm facing the worst part of myself and am finally comfortable enough not to try and annihilate it - but rather, I look at it with open curiosity. *Is this what I have been so afraid of?*

Because of this, everything that I have longed to express pours easily from my lips, "Lucas, you ruined my life. Every second of every day that I have lived has been tainted because a very long time ago I loved you. I regret ever having met you. You took advantage of me. You used me for your own gain. You stole paradise from me. I have survived, though, and I will continue to survive, but make no mistake; I see your face and I am reminded of the single biggest mistake of my life: *trusting you.*"

He takes another careful step forward, "If it's any consolation whatever pain I have caused you - I have experienced double for what I have done. I want to change. You are my only hope. If you can forgive me, I can start to live again, live the right way and make amends."

"And what about God?" My lip pulls in an indignant smile. "You once loved Him, as well."

Lucas sighs, "I don't know that I am ready for that. I was hoping to start with you. I just want the opportunity, Eve. I can see the suspicion in your eyes. Please just give me a chance to show you - not with my words, but through my actions. That is all I ask, just for the chance."

He doesn't cry, but I can feel his spirit weep. Compassion wells within me. I'm shocked that I can feel compassion for him. I try to shake it off, composing my cold resolution. "Are you scared to face the Creator?"

"Yes," he replies casting his gaze to the ground.

I step toward him, remembering the Creator's words to me in the garden, reminding me that I, just like Lucas was guilty and needed grace. He had told me that I couldn't expect any grace that I had not been willing to extend. In a moment of brave compassion I reach my palms for his. This surprises him.

I look into his eyes, they were bright blue eyes that were not the eyes of the Lucas that I had known, "I want to see you."

"It is me. I may be in human form, but it is me who stands before you."

"I can feel that it is you. But I want to see *you,* the angel that I knew so long ago. I want to see your face again," I say.

He hesitates. He looks so vulnerable. "I'm ashamed of what I have become. Won't you accept me as I am now?"

Why is he ashamed? What could have changed about him over the years?

"Don't be afraid. Whatever the case may be; I need to see *you.* I will not talk to the form that you have taken. It is a lie. I need to see the real you. No more lies, Lucas. If you want me to consider what you have to say, you must never hide from me again."

A tear streams down his cheek. He is silent. A long moment passes. "It is difficult," he says.

I am overwhelmed with empathy, but am not swayed. "The choice is yours. I can see that this is hard for you, but I will leave if you are not honest with me in all things."

He deliberates. Taking a step back, he breaks the physical contact of our hands, "I must dim the lights."

"If you must," I allow.

He walks to his desk and touches a button on the console of his telephone. The silver windows turn black. The only light in the office comes from the overhead chandelier. He takes a breath and exhales. Upon his exhalation he is transformed.

When I see him, I understand his hesitation in revealing his true form. He is a monster... like all of the pictures depicted of him in mythology. His once beautiful angel's flesh, inscribed with the very name of God has been altered, replaced now by a harsh, scratched script. Every ugly intention that he has had over the years is branded on his face for all to see. The edges of the script have dried and curled, forming scabs and scales. His once lustrous hair now lies in brittle patches on his head. His teeth have rotted from the energy of every hateful word he has uttered. His once muscular frame is now soft and malnourished. His shoulders, once erect with pride now fall forward, and his puffed chest – concave, his heart had withered from all of the hate directed toward him. I realize that *no one,* not one single person has tried to help him over the years. No one has directed a moment of praise, nor felt a moment of compassion for him. He has had the energy of hate and blame directed at him time and time again.

I am amazed how the energy of a curse can alter a being. The only thing that remains the same is his eyes. Yet, they now shine with sorrow and regret. Even so, I can still see the magnificent beauty under it all. His beautiful eyes in this ghastly form remind me of an animal caged. Of a beautiful spirit caged in the body of an ogre. This time, when the compassion rises in my heart, I do not suppress it. I allow it to flow, like an unbound river and I cry, for him, for myself, for the world. I cry harder than I have cried for many lifetimes. The numbness of my many years of living melts, and my tears release an eternity of misery. Nothing is held back, and nothing is left but my raw anguish.

I reach my hand to touch his. He recoils. His flesh is not healthy and the lightest touch burns.

"Oh…" I cry, harder this time. Lucas cries too. His tears fall along the planes of his face, restoring his angel's flesh in the path of his tears. I reach my fingers to brush the tracks of his tears and the energy from my fingers compounds the restoration of his flesh. *My love amplifies the healing process.* His entire cheek beneath my fingers is transformed to the once silvery white angel's flesh. I want to hold him, but know that I cannot. The pain would be too intense. My heart overflows with compassion, if I could I would restore him in an instant, but I understand that this would have to be a gradual collaborative effort. *He would provide the sincerity, I would provide the support.* One could not survive without the other. *Was I ready for that? Was I even willing? I would have to be willing to forgive him.* The answer swells in my heart, a resounding, *yes!* The *yes* wells inside of me, gentle as dove's wings and as sturdy as oak. I would help him, for his sake, for my own, and for the sake of the world.

"I see why you wanted to hide yourself from me. Oh Lucifer, Son of the Morning, how far you have fallen. It is much worse than I imagined. Why didn't you do something to stop this long ago?"

Lucas shrugs, his limp shoulders a pitiful cry for mercy. "I suppose it's much like the aging process for humans, it happened so gradually that I couldn't see how far it had progressed. An ache here, a pain there. It's not just my appearance that has suffered, the condition of my body and spirits are the same. This body is just a reflection of what I hold inside. It has been so long since I have felt what it's like to be in my true form, I suppose that I've forgotten what I once was. Spending this time with you, forced though it may have been, has restored me enough to remind me."

I knew that I didn't completely trust him, because words are easy to say. Even still, I knew that I must help him. I was both scared and hopeful. "Where do you propose we go from here?"

"I don't know where, or how, to start. It all seems so far gone, doesn't it?"

"It does," I reply somberly. "Are you sure that you aren't ready to face the Creator?"

"I can't, not now." He holds his arm up, "Won't you help me? I would like to see if I can fix that which I have broken."

"It would be much faster if you went to the Creator."

"Faster, but not easier. I can't face him, not yet. Will you work with me? See what we can do with O.N.E. Earth? It would be a way for both you and I to redeem ourselves; together, as it was the two of us that started all of this."

An unexpected well of anger rose within me, "I will not shoulder the blame with you, Lucas. You tricked me, even after, you have destroyed every remaining good thing on this Earth. I tasted the fruit, but the rest I will not take responsibility for, and I resent you for implying any differently. You are unbelievable."

He is taken aback, as if he had been slapped in the face. The energy of my words tarnish his healed patches of flesh. Seeing the harm that my flash of anger caused, I soften,

"Oh, Lucas, I don't want to hurt you. But you must understand that this is all your fault. I was young and impressionable, and you were wise and convincing. The only responsibility that I will claim is my youth. I made a mistake, but I did so unknowingly and unwittingly. You knew what you were doing all along."

"I didn't realize it would turn out like this. I, too, was young Eve. And selfish, and prideful, and wrong," he finishes, defeated.

"Well, yes, you were," I agree redundantly, surprised that he gave in so easily. "Since you don't want to go to the Creator what do you propose we do?" I ask again.

A glimmer of hope shines from his eyes, contained within this fleshed cage. "There is something that I want to explain, if you will bear with me. You'll understand its relevance by the end. My change of heart isn't a recent thing. It started many years ago as just as a thought. It was one thought that turned into a plaguing dialogue, that turned into the plan and the mission of O.N.E. Earth. I had figured out how to fix everything. I called my legion, explaining to them the change of course. I admitted to them that I was wrong, and that the misery on this Earth, as it is, is not a kingdom that I was prepared to rule. I begged for my fallen angels to take the course of healing the Earth and humanity with me. Ironically, most didn't agree with me.

"Just as I rebelled against the Creator, so did my legion rebel against me. They are filled with the desire for power, just as I was so many years ago. Only one third of my legion has taken the course of redemption with me. Most are employed by O.N.E. Earth. Within the organization, they have struggled to become pure enough to lead the humans that we come into contact with well. We have experienced many ups and downs, even so, we have made a difference. However, we've struggled to make the impact that we desire, which is, as you know, world-wide peace.

"Not only do we *not* have the numbers on our side, we are fighting against the very system that we implemented to perfection, as well as the generations of humans that have been raised under our system of influence. Humans brains have been literally wired to hold and pass down the illusions that we have bound them with," Lucas pauses, assessing my reaction to this information.

"I have something to tell you, but I can't bear to expose myself in this, form," Lucas says, as if disgusted by himself. "May I have your permission to merge back into my human form?"

"You may," I allow. I wonder what he will reveal to me. What possible thing could he share that would be worse than what I already knew of him? Lucas was never boring; I'd give him that. From the very beginning he had a way of captivating my attention, causing me to make allowances just to hear what he had to say next. In a blink of an eye he was transformed into the beautiful man that I met earlier that day. He seemed far more comfortable. He takes my hand.

"Lucas, it was hard to see what you have become, and I know it was even more difficult for you to show yourself to me, but I must insist that if we do – work together, if I do decide to help you, than you must reveal yourself to me daily, for your skin will not lie, as your lips would. I must see your true form in order to ensure that you are not deceiving me again."

Evan's handsome face smiles, "Yes, of course. I don't expect you to trust me, yet. Anything you require, I will do."

I smile. I can't believe that I am smiling at Lucas. *What had happened to me?* I spent lifetimes cursing him, and now, within hours of seeing him again I was smiling. I might regret this. I hoped not. "Continue. What were you saying?"

"Oh, yes." Lucas rubs his face, and runs his fingers through corn silk curls. He exhales. Seconds pass before he speaks again.

One. Two. Three.

This was an awkward pause.

He takes my hands, looks deep into eyes, "I have kept near you, all of your lifetimes, but was sure to never come into direct contact with you."

Waves of shock pass through my body. This information disturbs me. My mind traces over the years, looking for the slightest hint of his face.

"Don't be upset, please. Just let me finish, and you'll understand. You see; I did fall in love with you in the garden. I didn't know the extent of it until we were separated. I found that I couldn't live without you, but I couldn't be with you, because of the bond of marriage that the Creator created between you and Adam. Until you broke that contract, there was nothing that I could do to ease the pain of our separation, but to be near to you in the only way that I could. Near, but not with…" Lucas trails off.

I narrow my eyes, *"How near?"*

"Sometimes I was your neighbor, the quiet one that you never met. Sometimes the shopkeeper in your town. An adopted second cousin. The woman at the bus stop. Always watching, but unable to touch, unable to make any meaningful contact, as I would risk being found out."

I close my eyes and breathe, "Okay, Lucas. I'm need a minute." I breathe in and out, to calm myself. I feel violated.

"I needed to be near you. To see you. I tried to stay away for a couple of lifetimes, but I could still feel you, through our bond. Trust me, feeling you and not seeing you is much worse than seeing you but not touching you."

"You have been stalking me? That is unfair, and rude, and creepy…" I shiver.

"I have done much worse," he reminds me. Another long moment passes. "It did come from a place of love, though you may not be able to see that. Not seeing you created an unending anxiety within me. Stalking you… as you put it, was the only way that I could find a moments peace. I'm sorry, for everything, Eve. It was wrong. But there is more… will you let me finish, please?"

I sigh, "Go ahead." I can't look at him. My mind is numb from information overload. Suddenly, I find that I am too tired to comprehend what he is saying.

"I needed to be near you, not only to ease my own discomfort, but to also keep an eye on you, make sure that you were okay. In this lifetime, I knew that Adam was going to leave. I just knew it. I had watched his depression worsen for the last couple of lifetimes and knew that he would leave. My chance for redemption was near. I survived the rebellion of my legion, gained wealth and status in this human form, and started this corporation - all in preparation for this moment. I know that for you this moment is many things, many more bad than good, but for me, this is the moment that my life begins again. It is my re-birth. This is a very special moment for me, if not for you. The fact that you are so open and so much more gracious than I imagined, or deserve, well, it makes this moment that much more special for me."

I nod my head. What he said is true, Adam had one foot out the door for the past couple of lifetimes. He just wanted to live as a stockbroker in the suburbs, forget about who we were, and live a normal life, while I still burned with a passion to fix the world that I had created.

"I have one more confession to make. It will either make your skin crawl or you will see it as romantic. Do you want to know?"

"Ughh. What?" I roll my eyes.

"My name, Evan. It is a combination of your first name and what I hope is your last name. Eve and Anne."

Giving up, I laugh, draining the tension from me, "Creepy and romantic. But I must be honest with you, Lucas - I have no romantic intentions toward you. Really," I end, seriously.

"I can accept that. Romance can take many forms. You may not want me romantically, but even your friendship is enough for me. I promise."

A thought occurs to me, "Why did you wait for me? Why couldn't you restore the Earth on your own, and then come to me?"

He takes my hands again, "There is something magical about you. I know you feel it. There is something even more special about the combination of the two of us. You inspire me to be better than I am. When you were unattainable the difficulty of the task seemed insurmountable. Knowing that you will support me; that you will help me, motivates me. When I cried, you saw that my flesh was restored; when you touched my tears the restoration beneath your fingertips was a hundred fold. Without you, I don't know that I could do it. With your help my own process of healing will be accelerated - and as I heal, so will humanity." He rubs my palms with his thumbs, "I need you."

What he was saying seemed true, "What now?"

He squeezes my hands, "Go home. Process. Come back tomorrow and we will begin our plans."

I exhale. This has been a very long day. The connection that Lucas and I established has ebbed, "Alright, give me five minutes to get to my car before you unfreeze time. Once the motion of life starts again, if I am not ready, my car will be hit. I left it in the middle of the street."

"Your car is in the parking lot," he says.

"What?" I look around the room. He and I seemed to be the only two people who hadn't been affected by his trick with time.

"It has been returned," he assures me.

Too tired to question him, I allow his evasive answer. He escorts me to the elevator, pushed the button, and leans toward me,

"Thank you, Eve." He bows his head in gratitude.

"You are welcome, Lucas. I'm glad for your change of heart, really. I'm proud of you."

This takes him by surprise. The momentary shock on his face melts into a huge, blissful smile; the smile of a boy who has been given accolades by his mother. He hugs me until the elevator doors open.

"See you tomorrow?" he asks, hopefully.

My, how the tables have turned, I muse. He now looks at me with the same hopeful expectation that was in my own eyes when we were in the garden, "See you tomorrow, Lucas. When the sun is at its highest." They are the very same words that I spoke to him when we met in the garden.

Chapter 15

What have I gotten myself into? I must be crazy. I drive out of the parking lot. The motion of life around me has resumed. *Was this just another trick?* Lucas' change of heart seemed real, but then again so many things in my lives have felt real, good, only to have turned out badly. I wonder, how can we be expected to make the right choices when we only see life from our own perspective? How can we make decisions if we don't have all of the data we need? We walk around this world, expected to do the right thing, but we are blindfolded. Some would say; *Trust your heart* - but that has rarely worked for me.

I resolve myself to convince Lucas to go to the Creator and to end this horrendous game. He isn't ready now, I know that, but soon, with the right encouragement, he will be. He is obviously looking for my help. Perhaps all he needs is a little push in the right direction. He may not know that is what he is looking for, but I can influence him, help him have the courage to face the Creator. *Yes, I will help him be brave.* Of course, I will be wary, and of course, I will face any tribulation that comes my way, but I must convince him to restore himself, and thus myself and humanity. It is really the only thing that I can do. This is a once in a million lifetime opportunity, and I won't let it go to waste.

I'm surprised to find that I'm already home. I have no recollection of the drive, the traffic, of anything but my own thoughts. Once in my apartment, I pour myself a glass of wine. Nothing else seems appropriate. I rarely drink, but tonight is an exception. I'm craving the taste of wine. I sip the sacrament and am reminded of Jesus. My heart swells with appreciation and my eyes well with tears. I've had so many defeats in my life, so many lows, but I have also loved greatly. Loved deeper than I could have hoped for. Jesus, my dear Jesus. *How many lifetimes ago was it that our paths crossed?* Too many to count. And yet, his beauty is etched upon my mind. When I think of him now, he is tangible, right in front of me, more than a memory. Holding him all of those lifetimes ago, changed me. I was granted, for what seemed like only moments, the perfection that was intended for me in the garden, before the fall.

Losing him was another of the excruciating losses that I have endured. My greatest hope is to reunite Lucas with the Father so that our suffering may end once and for all. So that I may see the face of the Creator again, and Jesus, but most of all, so that I may see Adam's joyous smile, just as it used to be.

Chapter 16
The Beginning – Headquarters

Tens of thousands of angels stand erect in neat rows, perfect posture, in rapt attention. The air is still with a feeling of victory. Lucas walks onto the stage at the front of the grand hall, with its shimmering floors of mercury, the subtle movement of the floor creates the illusion that he is hovering just above the ground. Yet he stands still, grounded in the ownership of his space. The cool gray walls are an immaculate canvas for his luxurious black robes, fitted to his tall slender form. On the outermost robe, the image of a singular silver serpent slithers down the left arm. His chiseled face catches the light; he is impossibly beautiful. He wears his dark hair back, neatly tied in a knot. There is pride in his stance. He stands with the power of a warrior and the grace of a poet. Lucas takes a moment to look over his fallen legion. Looking over the crowd, face by face, he connects eyes with each of his brave revolutionists. After some minutes pass, he smiles. With hands clasped behind his back, he begins to comfortably, yet purposefully, pace back and forth as his address begins. Lucas' voice echoes, reaching the farthest of his subjects in clear tones,

"It has begun. Our liberation from the Creator. There is no turning back from here. Soon we will have this world for our own," Lucas finishes his sentence, emphasizing the point by raising his voice to a shout. In response, the crowd breaks into applause; laughter and exaltations.

As the exuberance dies, Lucas begins again, "You declared your independence today, you stood in the presence of the Creator with pride and no fear. You claimed your life as your own today. We have a large job in front of us. One that will take sacrifice, but one that is worth every ounce of passion that you put into it. The sacrifice is great, but the gain even greater. Our numbers are few, but our might is great. We shall achieve true independence from our oppressor! Lucas exclaims.

"In our world, there will be no consequences. We will be free to be who we are, as we are. In our world, we shall have everything that our heart desires, no limits, no rules, no archaic protocols or pecking orders. You shall be the king of your own destiny. No longer will you have to bend your will to another. No longer will you have to hope for the things that you desire to be bestowed upon you by some 'great distributor of gifts'. These will no longer be things that you have to pine for, beg for, and ask permission to have!" Lucas pauses, looking over the crowd thoughtfully.

"We have the power to make this happen, *you* have the power to make this happen. *Can you do it?* " Lucas questions the audience with sharp enthusiasm. The angels roar in a resounding "yes" and cheer loudly. Lucas smiles and continues, "The beings in heaven are distracted by their service to the Creator. We can use this to our advantage; exploit it as their weakness. Our allegiance is only to our mission. We must each individually take responsibility for, and control of, our fate. We will pay no consequence for what it is that our heart desires!"

Lucas face becomes serious, his tone turning to business, "It may seem that our immortality and our very existence are at stake. I assure you, they are not. We must work diligently, as life is no longer a gift, but our manifest destiny. We must be as clever as is the serpent, not dependent as the servant!" Lucas raises his fist in the air to punctuate his point. The crowd roars to life, louder than before. Lucas motions for the crowd to quiet and continues,

"I have put great thought into this and have come to the conclusion that we can use the life force of man and his creative energies to fuel our immortality, until we develop a source of our own. Your journey starts today; this is just the first step of many. You will tire, become weary, you will achieve and celebrate victory.

"And who shall rule our heaven, our Earth? We shall. Man will serve us. Man will work for us. And those that resist us? They shall be tormented, and shall curse the day that they were born, for we *shall* win, at any cost. Do not give those that offend us with their allegiance to the Creator a moment's peace. We shall show them as examples, examples of the consequence of being weak minded.

"We have much to do; you will all receive individual instructions based upon your talents to optimize your success. We shall begin our preparations tomorrow." Lucas' tone brightens, "But for tonight, well, tonight it is time to celebrate our victory and this great opportunity!"

The crowd responds with a roar of delight. Music plays, signifying the beginning of the festivities. Lucas, in closing, bows his head to the masses and exits the stage, his dark silken robes flowing like the dark blanket of eternity itself.

****

Youvanah, fallen angel whose name means "interferes with the divine will" leans in to whisper to Lucas, "Master, the twelve have gathered."

Lucas turns to Youvanah, whose bright blue eyes immediately lower in respect. She bows her head of cornsilk curls subordinately and raises her beautiful eyes to look at Lucas.

"Has everything been prepared for the ceremony?" Lucas asks easily, smiling at a passing angel who dances in celebration.

"Yes, Master all is set," Youvanah confirms proudly.

"Very good, let us go now," Lucas says.

"This way, Master." Youvanah motions for Lucas to proceed toward a hidden exit in the far left corner of the grand hall where the celebration is in full swing. She opens a nondescript black door; it swings open soundlessly, revealing a long hallway filled with a panoramic battle scene.

Lucas steps over the threshold and she quietly closes the door behind him, leaving Lucas to walk the long hall by himself. As he walks, Lucas studies each of the engravings that adorns the long space, the light from above giving life to the pristine array of three-dimensional silver angels' faces. The details of the engravings are exact, showing the battle-plan for the ages. At the end of the corridor the pictorial panorama comes to a climax. As Lucas approaches a door at the end of the passageway, he pauses to contemplate the scene depicted before him.

His Earth. He realizes that in the space beyond this sacred door he will achieve that vision. Moved, he closes his eyes to feel the supreme importance of this moment. He takes a breath to center himself and exhales deeply, placing a dynamic smile upon his face.

As Lucas steps over the threshold he is greeted by twelve expectant angel's faces, each sitting apprehensively around a long rectangular black lacquered table. The room is a comfortable, if dim. Black walls, dark marble floor, dark cathedral ceiling; the only light in the room the illumination emanating from the angels. They radiate a soft glow, each its own eternal flame. Seeing the questions in each angel's eyes, Lucas greets his guests.

"You are wondering why you have been pulled from the festivities," Lucas states, reading the curious expressions in the room. "You are here because you have each been chosen to hold an important position within our organization. Each one of you has been chosen to work closely with me to advance our cause. You are offered this honorable position because you possess the leadership, talents, and gifts that will be essential to the success of our mission. I have personally chosen you to be head of your own division. I expect that you will lead the angels in your charge well and achieve success. In this position, you will be remembered throughout the ages as the leaders of this great revolution… The *heroes* of this battle for independence."

Lucas' hands rise, revealing an ornate silver chalice; a silver serpent winds its way up the stem, it's head anchored to the body of the cup. Its long silver forked tongue ascends from the creature's mouth, wrapping itself around the rim. The tips of the forked tongue extend to a sharp point rising mere millimeters from the rim, sharp as a razor. The contents of the chalice shine brightly, illuminating the space above the cup with a cold white light.

"In this cup," Lucas pauses, "is the remaining light from the fruit of Pandora. The Tree of the Knowledge of Good and Evil is no more, but the light remains for us to partake. This invitation to drink of its power is an honor above all honors, for it is this light that will give you the power above all others. Taste it once and you shall forever be elevated above all. Taste the light of the gods and you accept your mission to lead us into victory!" Lucas holds the cup high above his head, "Drink this and you shall effortlessly be connected to the rhythm of life, as this light will bind you to the mind of man."

In demonstration Lucas brings the chalice to his lips. He punctures the tip of his tongue with the razor sharp edges of the serpent's forked tongue. A drop of blood appears. He smiles and takes a sip of the light. The entire energy of the room shifts and the wattage behind Lucas' flesh immediately intensifies a thousand times. Light beams out in strong definitive rays through the text engraved upon his flesh. His shining eyes beam light into the room around him. Each of the angels gasp as the power emanating from

Lucas hits them in waves. They too feel the power as the light within them surges simply by being in Lucas' proximity.

Lucas shouts, declaring in a mighty voice, "I am Lucas, *son of no one*. I am my own authority. I am a god, and future ruler of this Earth." Black robes, silver white skin, black hair, black eyes, cold white light shining brilliantly. Lucas is awesome and terrifying at the same time. His beauty unsurpassed, his elegance, strength and grace impossible to look away from. Twelve angel's gazes watch him with fascination, with awe, with respect, with envy.

Chapter 17
Present Day

At exactly twelve o'clock I step into the executive lobby of O.N.E. Earth. There is a lightness to my step, one that I haven't felt in years. *What is this lightness?* The answer comes beaming from my smile: *It is hope.*

"Mr. Stream is expecting you," the receptionist smiles, as if she is in on the secret. I look at her beautiful face and wonder if she is one of the angels that had fallen so long ago. I wonder if she too is a brave angel on her path to redemption. I meet her smile with one of my own.

"Right this way," she says, leading me to the door of Lucas' office. I step into his office without announcement, where he is waiting for me. When he turns around I see that his hands were mid-wring, as if moments ago he had been nervously pacing, waiting to see if I would show. This mental image brought a smile to my lips.

"You came," He says, crossing the distance to embrace me, relief washes over his face.

"I did," I exhale, conveying my uncertainty.

"I'm glad," he also exhales.

We stand in front of each other awkwardly, not knowing what to do or say next.

"Let's take a walk," Lucas offers, placing his hand on the small of my back. My flesh pulls toward his hand, like metal fillings to a magnet. There is something excruciatingly right about his touch. It is difficult to admit, but my flesh never pulled like this toward Adam. He never intoxicated me like this. The need was never so great. Most things on this plane of existence provided zero stimulation, and because of that I have become numb. Even though I smile, interact, and pretend to be engaged, a part of me is always asleep. Bored. Apathetic. But this touch woke me up, reengaged me in the process of living; it breathed life back into my body. Then how could it be forbidden? Or was it?

A very large part of myself wanted to let go of all concepts of right and wrong, transcend all of it, and just squeeze every ounce of pleasure from this moment. I want to hold him. Run my fingers through hair. Celebrate the reunion as if no time had passed, as if we hadn't endured a whole lot of bad in during our absence. I wanted to touch him, pull and tug, until this need felt satisfied. Instead, I walk carefully, feeling the warmth circulating from his palm into my lower back, memorizing every particle of energy that danced inside of my flesh.

When step outside, Lucas motions for me to look around. People walked busily, drove, talked on mobile phones.

"Can you see?" Lucas asks.

"Yes," I reply, observing the mass of menial that flowed around us in currents.

"Do you really see?" Lucas questions again, the note in his voice makes me question if I see what he is referring to.

"I see the everyday," I explain.

"Then you don't see," he says. "If you really saw what is in front of you, then you wouldn't be so cavalier. The light of awareness must have worked its way from your system already. Time covers all wounds, or so they say."

I turn to him, "What do you see?"

"The same thing a baby sees the day that it is born onto this Earth. Reality without the conditioned veils. As I said, time covers all wounds." He turns to me, "Eve, I need to know your level of commitment to changing the world once and for all. This cannot be something you play at. You must commit your whole being, your very life. I assumed that you still would be able to see, from when I opened your eyes to the truth before. But vision fades with age, in all ways it seems. You will be of little help to me if you are entrenched in the same levels of consciousness as the people we are here to wake up."

He pulls a glass vial from the inside his suit jacket, it glows like liquid light encased in crystal. He looks into my eyes with such intensity that my breath becomes short. In one movement he snaps the cap off with his thumb and turns the vial above my lips. My eyes go wide.

"Don't think, just drink," he says urgently.

"Lucas, no!" I protest.

But it was too late. One drop of the fruit of Pandora, the nectar from the Tree of the Knowledge of Good and Evil falls onto my lip. It burns and freezes at the same time. Currents of cool energy pulse through my lips, through my face, through all of the cells in my body, activating one after another, like dominoes. I hear a pop at the crown of my head, and again, like so many lifetimes ago, I feel an intense laser of cool energy pouring into my brain, stretching and recalibrating the physical mass inside, the sound of which is deafening.

I fall back, into Lucas' arms.

Again.

When I open my eyes, I close them immediately and scream, "No!"

Curling myself into a ball, I wrap my arms over my head in order to shield myself from what I saw. My heart tears, followed by each of my chakras twisting shut due to the shock. Complete system overload. Four additional levels of reality open into a sea of chaos. Demons everywhere. Energy being squeezed, siphoned, and knocked violently from each of the humans who walk along the street. They smile politely, enduring their bad days as best they can, oblivious to what is going on. Every horror show, every campfire story, every imagining of what goes bump in the night bustles along in a savage mid-day feast for these demonic beings, the humans unwitting lambs to the slaughter. My heart tears open with the realization that I created this world. With an intensity long forgotten I scream, "Stop!"

Like a shock wave, the violence of my exclamation sends ripples of vibration through the overlapping dimensions. All take notice, on all levels of reality. The humans look at me dumbly, not seeing what I see. Some are annoyed, some concerned, but all look at me like I am a woman on the verge of a mental breakdown. The demonic beasts snap their heads toward me, realizing that I see them, and begin to move toward me with impossible speed. In an instant we are surrounded. Twenty warriors of darkness jump toward me. Lucas fights off the closest of the beasts, smashing fists, hurdling, using the force of his body to push them away. I should be terrified, but I am not.

I am angry. Really angry. Without thinking, I launch my body into the mass of snarling beasts. If I die, it will be in a noble way. I will take out as many of these monsters as possible. Determination and power burn in my core. Moving easily through the additional layers of reality, I take on beast after beast, tearing eyes out, twisting necks, stepping on spines.

The savage has awoken within. My former role as victim was burned away by rage. I have been waiting for this battle for eons. My fist flies forward, penetrating the face of the monster in front of me. It falls to the ground, my fist still lodged in its face. When I pull back to release my hand from its confines, I lose my footing and fall backward. Three long talons swipe down, tearing the flesh on my face. Another talon pierces the top of my head. I am on the ground, surrounded. Two demonic hands pass through my chest, squeezing my lungs. Gasping for breath, sputtering coughs, I twist my body and maneuver my foot against the chest of the beast suffocating me and push with all of my might. Lucas tears me away from the clutches of the mounting beasts. I fight against Lucas, to no avail. He runs us to the safety of his office building.

"Put me down!" I yell, defiantly.

"This is not the time," he barks. When he pulls the heavy glass door shut, he chants something in his original tongue, and a field of energy seals the door of the office building behind us. Clamors from the unearthly beings echo behind us. I scream a stream of obscenities through the glass at them.

When Lucas sets me on the ground, I race toward the door, ready to launch myself into battle - but my hand cannot penetrate the field of energy. Lucas grabs my shoulders, spins me around and slaps me. The blow stuns me,

"You slapped me?" I huff, disbelieving.

He smiles, a little too easily, "You were hysterical."

My eyes narrow, "A little cliché?"

"Perhaps, but it worked," he smirks.

"Why won't you fight?" I ask desperately.

"This battle has been going on for ages. It didn't start today. Brute force is not the way. We are outnumbered. Without an army, we'll never win. But, there is a way."

"What?" I ask, verging on tears.

"The light of Pandora," he says.

"How?" I say, above a whisper.

"Mass distribution," he says, looking into my eyes.

Chapter 18
The Beginning

Lucas and I go to Adam. It is mere hours before the dawn. Adam is awake. When he sees me, a look of relief washes over his face.

"Where were you?" I was worried." He strides over and embraces me tightly. When he pulls out of the embrace he sees that Lucas has entered the shelter behind me. A look of confusion crosses his face, "Who's this?"

"Adam, this is Lucas. You remember, I told you about him. I've been with him all evening. I'm sorry that I didn't come home earlier, but I couldn't. Please, Adam, sit. We have something to tell you," I say.

Worry contorts his face, "What happened? Are you okay?"

I look directly into Adam's eyes, "Adam, let's sit. You'll understand everything soon."

Adam nods. We sit, the three of us in a circle, knee to knee. I introduce Lucas,

"Adam, Lucas is, he helped the Creator design this paradise for us. He has some information about the Creator that I think you should hear."

Adam looks at Lucas, appraising him. Lucas is magnificent; Adam takes in the heavenly contours of his form and nods, "Go ahead."

Lucas places his palms face up. I put my palm on his and offer my other to Adam. Catching on, Adam takes my hand and offers his other to Lucas.

"What I have to convey cannot be spoken in words. I'm going to show you something. You will see it in your mind. Please close your eyes," Lucas instructs.

A circuit of energy forms, from Lucas to me, then Adam. We are transported into the first vision that I had while sitting with Lucas at the water's edge. When the vision ends Adam opens his eyes and pulls back his hands as if they had been burned. Grabbing at his chest, he kneads - as if trying to massage away the pain. His alarmed gaze falls on Lucas. The contours of his face distorted by pain,

"What was that? What did you do to me?" Adam asks.

Lucas' reply is calm, his eyes filled with compassion, "You felt a possibility. One that if it should happen to you, you would not be prepared for. I hope that you can benefit from my experience and decide for yourself if you wish to risk the same fate. If the Lord denied me, then surely he shall do the same to you. You felt it yourself. It's up to you to decide if you would like to know more." Lucas retracted some of the power from his gaze, leaving Adam to sit with the feelings and information that he just received.

"Don't talk about the Creator that way," Adam warns.

"Adam," I reach my hand to touch his. "Listen to him, his experience speaks for itself. He can show us how to acquire independence, to be self-reliant. We would be like gods ourselves."

Adam looks at me sharply, "Eve, what are you saying?"

"I have seen more than you. I know that what Lucas is saying is true. We would be fools if we don't consider what he has to say. The same fate may await us, Adam. I think taking precautions for that not to happen would be wise."

Lucas puts his hand on Adam's knee, "There is more, if you would like to see."

"Okay," Adam says, his resolve fading. Adam looks to me for reassurance. I nod in approval. "Okay, tell me," Adam concedes.

"It's not something you can know with words. We'll have to go into meditation again. But, your mind is not prepared for the truth yet. There is something you must do first."

Adam is wary, he looks to me.

"Lucas, could you leave us for a moment?" I ask, "I want to talk to Adam privately."

"I understand," Lucas nods, rising to leave. "I'll return in a moment. We don't have a lot of time."

I nod. Once Lucas leaves, I turn to Adam, moving closer to him, "Adam, what Lucas suggests, we must do. I trust him. I have seen more than you and I know that he is right. If you do not trust him, then trust me," I say.

Adam takes my face into his hands, "Eve, I love you. I trust you, but Lucas' experience is not ours. We cannot gauge *our* fate from *his* experience."

Looking into Adam's eyes, I channel my love into him, "Trust me, Adam. If only for a moment. Please."

Adam looks into my eyes and says, "Alright, I'll see."

"Thank you, Adam. You won't regret it," I promise.

As if on cue Lucas returns. He walks into the room and sits near us. Between his fingers he holds a cube of light. When Adam sees the fruit, his eyes go wide. A look of sheer terror passes over his features, then he glares at me angrily, as if I have betrayed a thousand silent promises.

I hold my hand out for the cube of light; Lucas places the sacrament into my palm. Adam shakes his head, eyes fearful. I nod, "You must, Adam, without it you will never know the truth." I can feel the power from the fruit surging into my hand.

Adam, whispers, he is afraid that if he speaks too loudly somehow the Creator might hear, "Eve, God has forbidden it. If we eat it, we will die."

"I have already eaten it, Adam, and God has not even acknowledged that I have eaten it, much less punished me for it. It was a lie, Adam. Look at my face, I am here, I am still alive."

Adam is afraid; he shakes his head. Turning his attention to Lucas, Adam stands, seething, "You! You did this. I don't know what you want, but you have to leave, now!"

Lucas calmly assesses Adam's aggressive stance. He does not move an inch. He looks intently into Adam's eyes, "I did nothing. It was Eve's choice. She is the one you should question. All you have to do is ask and she will tell you why she has chosen to become enlightened to the truth."

"Get out," Adams voice lowers to a growl. Taking another step forward, Adam grabs Lucas' wrist and attempts to escort him to the door. Lucas does not budge. Adam strains with the effort, clearly out-manned.

"Adam, embrace your fate. If you choose not to join Eve in her enlightenment, she will leave you. If you choose not to eat of the fruit, you will have to live through eternity without her, and she will spend the eternity with me. She can be your queen or mine. The choice is yours."

Adam's face burns hot. He shouts, "You will pay for this. If you do not leave now, I will…"

Lucas interrupts, laughing, "You will what? You will force me to leave? You will cry and go tell the Creator?"

"Exactly," Adam steps back and grabs my arm roughly. "Let's go." Adam pulls me toward the door.

Lucas stops him with his voice, "Adam, how do you intend on doing that? Where is he now? Where is your beloved Creator? He has never shown his face before, what makes you think that he will come to your aid now? I am the only one here. It is I who has taken an interest in your life. It is I who offer you a new life."

"We don't want a new life. Once the Creator finds out what you have done, you'll be banished," Adam spits angrily.

"You forget that Eve has eaten the fruit already. If you take her to the Creator now - what do you think will happen to her? There is only one option for you, if you want to stay with her. You must also eat."

"If there is another way, *I* will find it!" Adam's face twists with rage.

"Adam! Adam, no!" I cry as I resist him. I can feel the power surging in the capsule, still clutched in my hand. The iced capsule is melting with every passing moment. Adam's eyes go flat; he stops and looks me dead in the eyes.

"Adam, just wait," I beg.

"Wait for what, Eve? There is nothing to wait for. Lucas lied to you. We must go to the Creator and beg for our lives."

"Adam, wait. You are not even considering what we are telling you. Be reasonable, please."

"No, I will not. Eve, we are leaving *now*." Adam pulls me through the doorway of our home. Striding with a single-pointed purpose, he leads us toward the Master's trees. I resist as he pulls me, slowing our pace.

"Adam, wait! You are hurting me. Stop!"

"I am not trying to hurt you, Eve. I am trying to *save* you. This is the only way that I know how, to get you away from *him*." Adam's face hardens.

In the distance the sky is illuminated, marking the path to our destination, the home of the sacred trees. The light around the clearing is bright as day, though night surrounds us with its deep charcoal cloak.

"Adam, you don't have to protect me from Lucas. He's not trying to hurt us, he's trying to help us."

"I do not trust him, Eve. I trust only myself."

"You don't trust me?" I ask, wounded.

"Not anymore," he says quietly. "You put your life into a stranger's hands. I'm going to try to save you, but I don't know if I can," desperation edges his voice. He is scared.

"Adam, you're overreacting. Lucas isn't a stranger to me, I know him. I have known him for quite some time. I believe him."

Adam stops cold, "Exactly how long have you known him?"

Oh. I forgot. I have kept my friendship with Lucas from Adam until only a day ago. My head drops, "For a while."

This time it is Adam who is wounded, "How long?"

"A while," I make my admission not with my words, but with my tone.

"Then you hid him from me? I should have never left you alone. This is my fault," he groans. Taking my hand, more gently this time, he pulls me behind him and over the threshold of the clearing. Lucas is already there, as majestic as ever. He stands between The Tree of the Knowledge of Good and Evil and the Tree of Life, blocking our view of the sun lit tree.

"Get out of our way," Adam sneers.

Lucas searches my face for answers, "Eve, this is your last chance for freedom. Everything that you have learned, everything that we have worked toward is at stake. Take another step forward and all will be lost. You must convince Adam what you know in your heart is right. Let him feel the fruit of Pandora. He does not need to eat it. He can feel it and have a preview of what we are offering."

I look at my palm. I still hold the sacrament that Lucas brought for Adam to eat. The skin of the fruit is much thinner now. "Adam?"

"No," he says.

"Why is it only you who decides what is good for us? I am affected by this, too. Please, just consider what it is that I want for a second. Respect my decision. You don't have to decide to eat of the fruit. You can just feel it. You can feel the power for yourself without tasting it. Here," I reach for his palm and place the fruit in the center. Adam looks at the cube with its glowing light circulating, shifting, and moving within the iced capsule

"Do you feel it Adam? That is the power of the truth. Taste it and you will no longer be in darkness. Taste it and you will understand why I have brought this to you."

Adam's eyes glaze as the overwhelming power in his palm overtakes his senses. Resolutely, Adam breaks from the trance, "I can't. I won't. What have you done?"

"Please, Adam trust me."

"No. I can't," is his final word. But it's too late. The thinning skin of the cube has melted from the warmth of Adam's palm; the light that escapes is immediately absorbed by his flesh. Adam flashes me one last look of alarm before his eyes roll into the back of his head. He falls back and his body begins to convulse. I reach for him, to break his fall. *The fall of man.* I hold him as his body and mind open. Finally, it stops. He is still. I stroke his face, knowing from my own experience what is happening inside of him. I look to Lucas, who smiles in encouragement,

"He'll wake soon," Lucas assures me.

I sink to my knees beside Adam's body and a tortured cry of lament escapes my lips. My conviction in the rightness of my decision fades.

"What have I done?" I look for answers in Lucas' eyes.

Lucas crouches next to me and places his hand on my shoulder, "You have done the right thing, Eve." He channels warm assurance through his eyes, "You'll see. You have done the right thing."

"Have I?" I cry, doubtfully. I want to trust him, but my faith is shaken by the tragic scene. "He didn't choose to eat of the fruit Lucas. He didn't choose…" I trail off, looking dumbly into the distance.

Adam opens his eyes. I can clearly see that he has been transformed. Time has stopped flowing as it normally had. There is a stillness in the air, yet we can see and feel the cosmic energies merging and swirling between us. When I look at his face, I can see the same ancient script inscribed upon it that had been on Lucas' face, revealing every private thought that he has ever had, every secret longing in his heart.

It is *my* name that is written on his face. Over and over again, I see only my name. He loves me with a depth that I had neither known nor imagined. Realizing that my face reveals more than I known, I look down, embarrassed, as Adam's name is not written in the same way on my face. When he looks at my face he will see my thoughts of the trees, the Creator, and Lucas. My heart is regretful. I am sorry that my dedication to him was not as great as his to me.

115

He doesn't seem to notice. He looks down at my body. When I follow his gaze I see what he is seeing. My body is beautiful. It has contours and curves I have never noticed before. There is a hunger in Adam's expression that awakens a fire inside of me. Instinctively, I lean forward and kiss him on the lips. He kisses me back, and we kiss in a way that we have never kissed before. Hunger. Longing. Fire.

A current of energy passes between us, heightening my senses. He consumes me, and I consume him with equal intensity. An intense sexual energy plays between us. I want to possess and be possessed in this heady moment that causes me to fall into the experience with an abandon that I have never known. Deeper, deeper, deeper, I fall. I cannot tell where Adam ends and I begin. We devour each other, our appetites insatiable. I lose myself in Adam. We have become one, merged ourselves, body, mind and soul. I forget about everything outside of Adam's touch. For me, this moment is all there is.

My attention is diverted, but only for a moment, when I hear Lucas' song coming from outside of the clearing. His song echoes through the garden. There is a tone of victory in his notes, of anger, jealously, passion, and regret. I wonder when Lucas had left, but Adam pulls my attention back; his mouth sucks at the flesh of my neck with a deep and passionate kiss. Adam and I share our first lovers' embrace until we fall asleep from exhaustion just as the sun comes up.

Chapter 19
The Mourning After

I am startled awake by sound of thunderous footsteps in the garden. Adam looks at me with horror. There isn't a sound in the garden but these footsteps. Everything else is still.

Terrified, I jump up without a second thought and run out of the clearing into the shelter of the orchard. I look around, there is nothing. It is safe, for now. Adam comes behind me fast. I grab his hand and start to run.

"Come on, let's go," I order. "We have to get out of here."

"Eve, wait!"

I turn around, casting an urgent look of warning, "Be quiet, Adam. He'll hear us. Lets go..."

Adam stands his ground, "Eve, we can't run. There is nowhere to go. We have to take responsibility for our choice, no matter how hard it seems."

"No," I protest.

Adam doesn't budge. His feet are solidly planted on the ground.

"Alright, you stay," I say, storming away. "But I'm leaving."

Adam chases me; grabbing my hand to stop me, "Eve, get control of yourself. We can't run from the Creator. There is nowhere to go. We have to face him and whatever consequences may await us. There is no choice."

I look down at my nakedness, "Adam, I can't let him see me like this, please, let me go."

Adam considers this for a moment, "I'll make a covering for you."

Determined, Adam marches over to a nearby fig tree. He begins weaving the long leaves together to fashion a covering, first for me, and then for himself. Once we are adequately clothed, Adam takes a long look into my eyes, "Remember Eve, this was your choice. I will stand by you, no matter the consequence. No matter what, we have each other." He smiles, trying to reassure me. It convinces neither one of us.

We turn and solemnly, hand in hand, walk west, toward the center of the Garden, knowing that the Creator is there under The Tree of Life. As we approach the clearing, my footsteps slow with dread and my heartbeat quickens. *Where is Lucas?* I silently will him to come to our defense. Adam squeezes my hand in encouragement as we enter the clearing. *He is so brave.* He shows no sign of fear, only regret. My admiration for him grows as does his beauty in my eyes.

When we step over the threshold of the clearing, we step into a force field of warmth and love. I can see each molecule of air singing and dancing in the golden light that emanates from the Creator. It is as if they bask in celebration of our special guest.

The Tree of the Knowledge of Good and Evil stands barren next to the Creator; the fruit of Pandora is no more. The now lifeless tree's branches, that once stood so proudly, droop in regret for holding the fruit that caused us to sin.

The Lord sits under The Tree of Life. His sits in the lotus posture, eyes closed. A celestial breeze blows his long hair of white, the purest white that I have ever seen. As the breeze blows each strand of hair shimmers, all of the colors of the rainbow are reflected in it for a moment, then it is white once more. He wears fine white robes that absorb and refract the light around him. His face is eternally young and impossibly handsome, a perfect peach that glows in golden light. Each of his pores is like the sun itself, beaming life into the space around him. His face looks just like mine, yet it also looks just like Adam's. He is the source, the original parent. Our Father.

Light as a feather, Adam and I fall forward, to our knees then to our faces. It's an automatic bow, not done consciously. Our bodies naturally yield to His magnificence. However, had my body delayed even a moment, I would have chosen to do the same. I weep tears of joy at the feet of my Father. Waves of awesome and complete love come from him. Wave after wave melts my body, mind, and soul into everythingness.

I hear birds flying in the air above me, and sense all the animals of the garden silently gathering around the clearing. All have come to peek at the face of the Creator and to offer their reverence and respect. They surround us, bowing to the Creator, accepting the gift of his presence. There is no other moment than this. No past, no future, just the wondrous all-consuming Now. I lie there, exhausted, yet energized. I am emptied of everything that is me and energized with the power of his majesty's love. I wish for this moment to never end. I could spend my entire life here on the ground, never raising my head, if only I could just be here with him, my one true love. I can feel the Lord retract his energy, just a bit. The power that held me to the ground in reverent love rises, so that, I, too may rise. I lift my eyes to see his face once more.

God opens his eyes and looks within me. In response every cell in my body dances with glee. He moves his gaze to Adam, looking into his soul and nods his head. He speaks to the animal kingdom that has gathered to pay their respects,

"Please, leave us now," he says. His voice surrounds us in supernatural stereo. He waves his hand, dismissing his beasts. The animals make their silent retreat. "Come," the Father says, patting his knee.

Adam and I rise to our feet. I am the first to climb onto one of the Lord's massive knees, and Adam follows. We melt into his shoulders, resting our weary souls. *I am home*. I feel as if I have been on a long and treacherous journey and now, here in the lap of my Father, I can finally find rest. I know the irony in this, I have been in a paradise that the Father had created to perfection. But I knew that where there was distance between me and the Creator there was no perfection, no matter how *perfect* it seemed.

I want to tell him I was sorry, I want to confess what I have done. I want to tell him that I have been a fool, and that I will never do something so horrible again. I want to tell him that I love him, but I cannot not speak, for I am too content to utter a single word. It is the Father who speaks first,

"Why did you hide from me?" He asked.

It's a simple question, but one that I cannot not fathom. *Had we hid from him?* Yes, I suppose that we had. While I contemplated it, Adam answers,

"We were afraid, my Lord."

The Lord asked, "Why would you be afraid?"

"We have done the unthinkable and we were scared to face you. But now…" Adam pauses uncertainly.

"Now, are you afraid?"

"No," Adam answers.

My mind is still numb from *the presence*. I am content not to speak.

The Creator asked, "What is so terrible that you wouldn't want to be with me?"

I bury my head deeper into the holy garment that clothes our Lord. The scent of him is indefinable, yet ever-present. That impossible scent, the scent that smelled like nothing and everything at the same time. *What was it?* I could detect notes of sunshine, earth, rain, peppermint, something sweet too, lemon, maybe? No not quite, closer to honey. The Lord pulls his shoulder back to gaze at my face,

"Eve, what is this thing that is so terrible that you would be ashamed for me to see you?"

"Father…" I cried. I cry, but I know not why. I know that I had been ashamed and afraid before, but I do not feel those things now. All that I feel now is ultimate love and peace. I curl deeper into him. He allows us to sit in silence, a moment to experience His love.

After a moment passed, he asks again, "Eve, what is it that you have done?"

"We have eaten of the Tree of the Knowledge of Good and Evil, my Lord," I confess.

The Father is quiet, "Was this paradise not enough for you?"

"It was," I say, "but Lucas, he deceived me. For after meeting him, I thought there was something greater than you. But I see now, Father, that is not so."

The Father turns to Adam, "And you, did you also eat of the fruit?"

When he looks into the Father's face, his own face absorbs the golden light emitted, and glows, although his features also show his sorrow, "I didn't eat it, but the light came in through my hand. It was Eve, Lord, she, tricked me," Adam says quietly, as if he didn't want to condemn me, but was unable to conceal the truth.

"I see," The Father says.

"It was a mistake, Lord. Is there any way that you can forgive this? Can things go back to the way they were? It was my mistake, not Adam's," I plead.

"And what of Lucas? What should I do with him?" He asks.

I cannot respond. *What was right? What was the right thing to do?* I am angry with him, for deceiving me, but it is difficult to condemn someone in the presence of such grace. But Lucas himself, he did not want to be with the Creator. That was his choice. Finally I answer, "Lucas has made his choice."

The Lord contemplates what I have said, "So, then, I should turn my back on him?"

Quietly I answer, "If you must, my Lord."

"Then, should I turn my back on you, Eve? You ask for grace but you do not propose that I absolve Lucas from his error, as well?"

I don't know how to answer. I am confused. "I see what you mean, Lord, but…" I can't find the correct words to speak.

"Lucas made a choice. You made a choice. Even Adam made a choice. He could have tossed the fruit from his hand the moment it touched him, but his hesitation cost him his life."

"*My life?*" Adam gulps, wide-eyed. "So it's true, we will die?" Adam looks at me pointedly, as if to say *I told you so*.

"You will die a thousand deaths, my dear one. Every day you live, you will die a little more. You will wish for death, but it will not come. That is the consequences of your error. However, you shall live again, I promise you that. Once you have worked until your fingers bleed and your heart can take no more, then you will have proven your desire to be with me above all else, and you shall live again."

"I will do it Lord," Adam says bravely. "Whatever it takes."

"I know you will, Adam, your heart is pure. You will make many mistakes, but I can see that your purity will remain." He turns his attention to me. "You, my daughter, you will have an even more difficult time than Adam," He warns. "Because your mind is easily deceived. You will not see the wolves in the sheep's clothing until the wisdom of many hurts gives you discernment. Your heart is equally as pure, but your mind is weak. You see goodness where there is none. That weakness will be taken advantage of. It will break your heart again and again. However, you will prevail in the end as a warrior for love. Your heart will be strengthened and you will have a mighty will and a great love. This I promise you. You will suffer, but your beauty and strength will grow to astounding heights."

Hearing of the struggles that I will face from the Creator sends me into a deep dread, but the Creator's confidence in me is a beam of hope. I look directly into the bright face of the Lord, etching every detail of this moment deeply into my soul.

He speaks again, "Eve, I ask you this so that you may know your own mind, and thus your own weakness. Why were you so easily deceived by Lucas?"

Why was I? My mind could not come up with a clear answer. There was a vague recollection, but I could not access the answer. "I don't know, Father," I admit.

He speaks to me with gentle authority. "Until you know this, you will know no rest. The key for you to overcome any struggle is to understand your weakness. Let this be the thing that you contemplate daily in your meditation. Why did you not trust in my greatness? You were impressed with the fleeting power of he who deceived you. *It is because you wanted something.* When you figure out what it was that you wanted, you shall understand yourself. And when you understand yourself, you will overcome yourself. This will make your redemption easier. Without asking that question, you can't know the answer."

"Lord, it wasn't that simple. I loved Lucas. I saw the tenderness of his heart. I don't understand why he would deceive me. I could *feel* his love. I just don't understand…"

"I know, Eve," he strokes my face. "For you it is difficult to see the motives behind the action. Love is a glorious thing, but do not be swayed by your emotions. Where there is love, there is no fear. You ate of the tree because Lucas' fears swayed you. You felt compassion and identification with him so your mind was not clear enough to make the decision that was best for *you*." To punctuate his point he drops his head forward, his forehead touching mine. My mind is filled with light. I feel myself expand further into - *what was further than eternity?* That was where I am.

"The lie that Lucas told you is that you could live and evolve without me. I am the ultimate teacher. I would have shown you all these things, and more, if you would have trusted me. One day, we shall once again be together in form. You must collect the portions of your mind that were fragmented throughout the Universe when you tasted the fruit. But again, Eve, you do not need to worry about how, as you will be shown every step of the way. Let your intention always be your reunion with me, and the outcome shall indeed be that reunion. Keep your heart on me at all times and your heart shall lead the way," He promised.

"I will." I vow. Then, having a moment of doubt, I ask, "Did you really abandon Lucas?"

The Lord sighs, "As you saw in your vision, Eve, I did not abandon him. Lucifer, in his jealousy, closed himself to my love. I cannot channel where there is no opening. I gave Lucifer free will. He did not trust the honor of the position that he held in the heavens and he could not understand why he was not chosen to rule this planet.

"I will tell you why I choose you; when I created you, I gave you a soul - here," he points to my chest. "I anchored my life force into you, so that I may rule and experience individuated life through you on this Earth. You and I are one and the same. I did not choose Lucifer to rule this planet because as the Creator it is my duty to do so, through you. I chose to experience this remotely though your eyes, through your heart, through your experiences. This is the highest honor, one that I have never bestowed upon any of my creations. You are my vehicle, my vessel to experience myself.

"The light of Pandora, from the fruit of The Tree Knowledge of Good and Evil, can act like a parasite to a vessel that is not great enough to consume it. It is a light that you are not equipped to filter or handle, so it became distorted. If you feed this parasite by making choices that nourish it, you give it power and it will grow. It will eventually take over your life. You will literally be a prisoner in your own body. If you starve those desires, it shall die and I shall live once again."

A question occurs to me, I ask, "The Tree of Life was in the garden when Adam was created, Lord. Why was this tree of deception placed in the garden when I was created? Am I evil?"

The Lord laughed, a mighty booming laugh, "No, Eve, you are not evil. The Tree of the Knowledge of Good and Evil is not evil nor is it good. The light of the Pandora is merely a drop of cosmic awareness. Lucifer, through his intention altered the light contained within, infusing it with his beliefs about me and the nature of life. By eating it prematurely the intended balance of the human was distorted.

"Do not misunderstand, knowledge is a positive thing and not to be feared, when you are prepared to handle it. If knowledge comes prematurely, without experience, then it can be distorted and misused. For this reason, this tree would be forbidden to you. When the time was right, I would have invited you to eat of the fruit and your body would have gone through a great transformation. You would have had the capacity to hold all of the mysteries of the Universe and all knowledge in your mind without distortion. You also would have had the power to create, just as I do. No other beings in the Universe can do that. Some can manipulate energy, transform it, but none can create energy out of nothing as I can. That was to be your destiny.

"As for The Tree of Life, it was my plan for part of your evolution. The tree carries the very essence of life, of my power. With the Tree of Life's presence in the garden, all life expands and grows. All beasts have kept their distance from the tree because their bodies are not equipped to stand in proximity to my power. You, on the other hand, were created to absorb that power, accumulate *the very essence of life* into your body, gradually, until your body became strong enough to handle the full mind of God. The universal mind is vast, this knowledge great; it takes a large and refined vessel to both receive and hold such great energy within it, without the knowledge becoming distorted.

"The fruit on the tree was a gift for Adam to eat once," the Lord smiled when he felt the waves of Adam's surprise. He continued, looking at Adam, "Yes, I said *eat*. The fruit was your gift to eat once your body had accumulated the energy necessary from being in its proximity. Your body was not prepared to ingest such a powerful force of energy yet, but it would have been if you would have just been patient.

"The Tree of Life was created as a portal between my world and this. It was my intention that Adam would not only be filled with my power with this tree, but communicate directly with me through this tree. There is a duplicate of the tree in my court inside of the sun.

"The first night that Adam came to The Tree of Life, Lucifer was in the heavenly court with me. Lucifer was angry, stating that Adam had done nothing to prove his worthiness to be the ruler of this planet. At that exact moment, we were surrounded with Adam's voice, transmitted through the tree. With his prayer he made a vow never to eat of the fruit of The Tree of Life, as he could feel its power. Adam did not think himself worthy to eat the fruit that I had made for him, thus proving his worthiness. In Adam's next breath however, he expressed a discontentment in the paradise that I had created for him, requesting a companion.

"Upon hearing this Lucifer implied that Adam had validated his point. Lucifer accused man of not being content with my creation or the gifts that I offered. I want you to understand that wanting companionship is not a sin, but Lucifer - determined to make his point, argued that Adam was not worthy because he asked for more than was given. Lucifer proposed that I give Adam the companion that he asked for. However, he challenged me to make man prove his worthiness before receiving the planet to rule. He proposed that I place The Tree of the Knowledge of Good and Evil in the garden and forbid the consumption of it.

"If Adam was content with my initial gift of life, and a companion, and wanted no more, thus trusting the wisdom of what I give and when I decide to give, then the tree would never be touched." The Lord turned his gaze to me, "If either you or Adam wanted more than I offered - you would eat of the fruit. This choice would result in me rescinding my decision to give this planet to the humans and you would be lowered from rulers with the potential to create to mere beasts.

"If you ate the fruit of Pandora, more energy would exist in the upper charkas, specifically the sixth, which is located in the center of your brain. Without your body being properly prepared the imbalance would cause distortion, confusion, struggle, and insanity. Lucifer challenged the perfection of my creation and your worthiness to hold the honor to be my direct descendants. He is very jealous of the potential that you hold.

"I saw an opportunity to right the dissention in the heavens, so, I accepted Lucas challenge, but I assured him it would not be as simple as he suggests. The terms of my agreement would be that, if the fruit were to be eaten, then you would experience what it is like to live in separation from me, to follow your own direction and whims and see where it takes you. You would also see what it is like to listen to my voice, trust me and live in harmony with me. You would experience both of these things based upon your intention. You would be offered the choice, daily.

"I would never, ever turn you into beasts based on one decision. Continually you, and your descendants, will decide; live with me inside of your heart or live without me. The determination of this will be based on how you live your lives. It is your choice. Reach for me and I will reach for you. Desire freedom from me by ignoring me and I will not claim you as my own. Very simple.

"You will either live with me as your king, the king inside of your heart. Or with Lucifer as your external king. With me, as it is me who lives through you, you will be the royalty of the Earth. With Lucifer, you will merely be a beast at the whim of your Master. A Master may love his dog, but that is all that being is to him, a dog.

"You are a part of me, and more precious to me than you will ever know. This challenge you and your decedents will face, will last a finite amount of time. You and Adam will live many lives. With each lifetime you will die in old age and be born again, immediately, into your next life. *You will be born into each lifetime with full knowledge of your previous lifetimes, all of the way back to the first moment of your initial creation in the garden.* All of your experiences and wisdom will be available to you; so that you may not forget why it is that you live. I give you this opportunity to be able to directly influence the outcome of the Lucifer's challenge, as it was your choice that began this game.

"Your descendants shall live only *one* lifetime each. Based upon how your decedents choose to live, their life will cast one vote; determining who shall rule the Earth in the end, Lucifer or me. At the moment of one's death a review of all of that persons intentions will be analyzed and at that time it will be determined in what direction their life's vote should be cast.

"Once the result of the challenge is determined, then you and all of your decedents shall be born again to live in the kingdom of the victor eternally.

"If Lucifer has earned more support, and thus lives, by the end of the fixed amount of time, this world shall be his. I will turn my back on humanity and give my creation for Lucifer to rule. The implications of that are grim, as it is my kingdom that powers all life on Earth. It is my kingdom that this Earth revolves around. You would have to advance against nature and discover an alternate power source. If Lucifer were to have his way, the sun would be blotted out and life on this planet will drastically change. However, if more souls reached for me as their king then the paradise that I intended for you shall be restored. At that time Lucifer will return to the heavens and once again live in harmony with me. All will be re1stored to my original desire.

"That is why I agreed to see this challenge through. I want to restore harmony in the heavens and put Lucifer's desire to be the ultimate ruler of this planet to rest," the Creator explained.

"How can we make sure that our decedents choose you?" I ask desperately.

"Teach them. Show them that they are themselves kings. It is inside of you that my throne on this Earth resides. Do not forget your royalty. Do not allow your decedents to forget their royalty. Lucifer will try to get you and your descendants to serve something outside of themselves - that is where his kingdom is. *He will have to teach the ways of his kingdom. They will only have to remember mine, as they already know them intuitively in the recesses of their hearts, as I am already there.* No matter how tired you become, or how bleak the situation, if I am your intention that will always be where you will be led."

Adam, who has been quietly contemplating our conversation, finally speaks, "If Lucifer is evil, why do you want to have him back in the heavens? Why put us through what seems will be a hell, for one fallen angel. It doesn't make sense."

God turns to Adam, "It's true, Lucifer has closed his heart to me, and that is the definition of evil, however, all hope is not lost. Lucifer has a great capacity to serve in love. It is my desire to restore him to that. You, yourself, closed your heart to me when you held the light of the tree. Even after that, your feet did not run you to The Tree of Life, which would have been the antidote to the poison of light to your mind. Instead, you stayed with Eve, and worshiped her body, something outside of yourself.

"What you experienced last night was something that I had been saving for you. I was to marry you and Eve, and on your wedding night, that was to be your gift. Once again, you could not wait for me to bestow my beautiful gift; you tried to take it before it was given. It seems that you and Lucifer have more in common than you realize."

Adam lowered his head, "May we take the antidote now?"

The Father looks at him with compassion, "I'm sorry, my son. The effects of the light spread too far throughout the recesses of your mind. What is done is done. If Lucifer is restored, you shall be restored, and if you are restored, Lucifer will be restored. This game need not be played, if Lucifer's heart opens to me once again before the challenge has been completed. *In a moment, everything can change.* Taking the light has bound your mind to him. He must either pull back the poison, or you must work it out of your mind with devotion.

"Since Eve actually ingested the light her struggle will be greater in restoring the proper balance of energy within her body. Adam, you will also have a difficult time, but you are in a far better position. Please, take care of her, help her along the way. She will need you more now than ever.

In our last moments here, in this paradise, I shall give you the gift that I intended for you. You and Eve shall be married, if you desire. I will marry your souls, so that each time you incarnate on this Earth you will find each other.

If you choose this, you will not be alone; you can find the strength to continue in each other. This will be my final blessing. Do you wish for this gift to be bestowed?" the Lord asked.

With tears in my eyes I nod my head, when the Lord looks to me for an answer. He then looks to Adam, who also nods. The Father puts a hand on each of our heads, "Do you Eve, promise to always find, encourage, and love Adam, throughout all of time?"

"I shall," I vowed with my heart.

"And do you Adam, promise to always find, encourage, and love Eve, throughout all of time?"

"I shall," Adam says, looking me deeply in the eyes.

The Father closed his eyes and infused an eternal bond between us. I could feel the very structure of the cells of my body being rewritten with this vow. It was now Adam and I; come what may.

"Your journey is long, my children. Choose well and we shall be together once again," the Father promised.

"It's time?" I cry tragically, with tears in my eyes.

"It is time," The Lord spoke.

Chapter 20

"Eve, look at me," Adam implores.

I rest my head in my hands, overwhelmed with grief.

"Just talk to me, please," he tries to engage me again.

I don't know what to say, so I sit there mutely. Since tasting the fruit of Pandora my senses have been heightened to excruciating levels. I find it difficult to focus on anything outside of myself because the energy of life swirls around me too quickly, deafening with its pace. The breeze in the trees, the rays of the sun, ants marching: two by two, the wind against my skin, animals emoting, my thoughts, Adam's thoughts, everything.

I am aware of everything; all life, all interaction, all at once, all of the time. It is too much. A never ending kaleidoscope. Too much to comprehend. Too much. I am going mad, I fear. I can feel the life in everything around me fading. The garden, once lush, illuminated with the forces of undiluted life is dying. Adam is dying, I am dying. Slowly. Every day, every second life dissipates, drifting upward toward the sky, like dust carried away by the wind. I can hear the plants mourn as their life force is depleted. I can feel agitation in the animals stir their restlessness. I can feel myself withering. Every day I wake and find Adam's face aged another day. We are growing older.

Adam's concerned eyes make this no better. His concern, meant to soothe, is yet another burden placed upon my shoulders. Without the Tree of Life in the Garden manifesting life - my bones ache and my heart cries. Adam's voice interrupts my wordless lament,

"Eve, darling. Please?"

I look at his face for but a moment. Shame immediately casts my eyes downward. I wouldn't be able to see him anyway, my eyes are always filled with tears. Without a word I stand. Without looking back I walk to the door. I step over the threshold and mumble three indiscernible words,

"He is gone."

I walk through the cemetery of our life, once so bright and vibrant, remembering. *No. Don't remember.* - I warn myself. Walking through the garden, as painful as it is to feel the consequence of everything I have done, is still strangely comforting, for at least I am alone. I trace my fingers over the leaves of the trees as I pass by and can feel the prick of death beneath my fingertips. The sun warms my flesh, but inside an artic chill circulates my spine. *Why am I always so cold?*

My feet lead me past the clearing. I bring myself to look in the direction where the two trees once lived. I find myself at the edge of the pond where Lucas and I met so many times before.

The water was the only thing that remained the same. *The water was the only thing that life did not leak from.* It was exquisitely neutral. It was the only place where my mind could find reprieve from the deafening cry of death. I submerge my body in the coolness of the water. My skin pricks as hairs raise, flesh feeling as cold as I do on the inside. I try to sink myself far below. It is quiet. I find a fleeting peace until I am buoyed to the surface once again.

When my head breaks the water my reflection gleams upon the mirrored pool, the mistakes of my past etched upon the planes of my face. I am too ugly to bear. The tide of my anguished indifference abated revealing what lies beneath, self-loathing for my foolishness. My stomach turns when I see my face in the reflection. I am disgusted. Muscles tense and fury releases adrenaline in a sudden rush.

"What is the matter with you? Why are you so stupid!" I scream at my reflection. With everything in me, I slash at the water with my fists. The water gives, waves splash into my face.

"I hate you!" I scream, thrashing my body in the water.

I try to wash the script from my face. Waves settle and I see that the script remains, shining out Lucas' name in words of light. If only I could erase my stupid thoughts, my stupid trust, my stupid obsession from my face, maybe then, I could look at Adam again. Roughly, I grab a porous rock from the floor of the pool, scrubbing my face until it hurt.

"I'm sorry! I'm sorry… just come off, please?" I cry, pressing harder.

"Eve! *What are you doing?*" Adam appears, rushing into the water, grabbing the rock from my hands. I struggle with him. I can't stop until every last word was gone.

"No!" I cry.

He takes the rough stone from me forcefully, "Eve! Stop!"

"No!" I cry. "I need it. Give it to me," the words pour from my lips as I fight for the object that he has taken from me. He tosses it into the center of the lake. Desperately, I reach down to the sanded floor, searching for a replacement, but find none.

Adam's strong arms pull me up. I fight him every inch of the way. He holds my body above the water. Kicking and screaming, I try to release myself from his constrictive hold. I knew that I was not acting as a sane person would. I didn't understand why I was behaving this way, I just felt impassioned, and angry and desperate. I was observing my behavior with a feeling of indifferent curiosity. Only half of me was thrashing about in Adam's arms, the other silently observing. I felt as if I were in a dream.

"Eve! Stop it!" Adam cries desperately. He carries me to the shore, pinning me beneath his body, holding my arms to my side. I fought him until exhaustion claimed my body and mind, until I was too tired to fight anymore, finally giving up and laying mutely. Seeing the damage that I had done to my face, Adam cries helplessly, brushing my wet hair from my face. He holds me, turning my body so that our eyes meet. I look away. I cannot look at him; it hurts too much. Adam shakes me hard,

"Look at me!" he says, frustration cutting his words. *"Eve. Please?"*

The desperation in his tone urges my eyes to his. Tears run down his face, stinging my wounded flesh. He looks as if he has absolutely no idea what to do. His warm brown eyes plead as he leans in slowly and kisses my lower lip, pulling it into his mouth with a tender and true kiss. I soften. I accept him, yielding, returning the tearful kiss. I was afraid to show my vulnerability, afraid to reveal my naked anguish to him with my words, but with this kiss, this tender cry for forgiveness, I expressed everything that words were not adequate to say. In this kiss I expressed my sorrow.

He pulls me into him, holding me tightly, stroking my hair, assuring me that everything would be okay. Strong arms that promise to take care of me in this dark hour. An overwhelming sense of gratitude fills me. The tears that fall now are different. They are not the tears of shame, no longer tears that alienate, but rather, tears that unite. These tears that I cry are tears that receive a love undeserved.

I look at Adam's face openly. I appreciate him more now than ever. He continues to stand by me, though I am becoming more complicated by the day. I cannot help myself. I wish that I could be better, for him. Stealing a glance at the sides of his face I notice that the words of light are obscured by streaks of mud that have dried upon his face. The color of the dried soil matches the tone of his skin exactly. I am inspired with an idea,

If I cannot scrub the sins from my face, perhaps I can cover them. I am filled with a sudden rush of hope. Yes, this is a very good idea.

Chapter 21
Present Day

"Mass distribution?" I echo Lucas' words.

The lobby suddenly got a lot bigger. I feel small, like a little girl in the center of an endless white room. "Drinking that light was the single biggest mistake of my life. What you are proposing is unthinkable. I will not even consider it."

Lucas takes my hand, places it on his chest, "It's the only way."

"I can't make that choice for them," I protest.

"You don't have too. We can distribute it to only those who want it," Lucas assures me.

"If they knew the doors that it would open, no one would ever take it," I cast my eyes to the windows, where the demons clamor at the door.

"Not a single person would forge any journey if they knew the trials they would encounter. The first step would never be taken. The hope of the result is what starts every journey. This is no different. We will tell them where it will lead, not the obstacles they will encounter on the way," he says.

"Just like you did with me?"

"This is different."

"Seems the same. Only this time I am on the other side."

He considers my answer. Trying again, he says, "Are you prepared to live your life continuously seeing the feeding that you saw today? We are almost at the end, Eve - you can't turn back now. You have to liberate them."

I feel like I am on hanging on a branch that dangles precariously over a cliff, an endless abyss below. I'm afraid that the branch will break and I will fall. My body shakes with terror.

Without me speaking, Lucas answers the thought, "What you don't realize is that if you just let go, you will find that you can fly."

"Things have changed since I last took the fruit of Pandora. Taking the fruit was a glorious experience in the garden. It's a different world now. They wouldn't last five minutes with that type of awareness. It would be like waking up to a nightmare."

"Would you rather them stay asleep?" he asks. "They are your children, of course, I won't do this without your consent. But remember the end result. There is a very real possibility that humanity, as a whole, can take back their power to live their lives. We just have to show them their oppressors."

I look around the room, desperately, "Nobody else knows? No one else can see?"

"The unlucky few that do isolate themselves onto mountain tops, or end up in psychiatric wards." He takes my hands, "It's a hard choice, and I am sorry to put you in this position, but it is a choice only you can make. Will you wake them up?"

"Enlightenment is a bitch," I grumble.

"Indeed," Lucas agrees.

The choice whether to keep my children at a comfortable level of numbness while I try to single handedly take on legions of demons, or wake them up abruptly to a war that they didn't know existed, awakening many allies in this fight for freedom. One is too big and too slow, the other too harsh and cruel.

Chapter 22

I stand before a mass of media as a representative of the World Health Organization, Lucas behind me on the left, a representative from the United Nations on my right. I step to the microphone and begin my address, the tin of my own voice echoes through the speakers in my ears.

"The world is now at the beginning of a pandemic. This pandemic must be taken seriously precisely because of its capacity to spread rapidly to every country in the world. All countries should immediately activate their preparedness plans. This high phase of alert is a signal to governments, ministries of health, and other ministries that certain actions should be undertaken with increased urgency at an accelerated pace. The international community should treat this as a window of opportunity to ramp up preparedness and response.

Vaccinations will be available to the public as early as tomorrow at distribution centers in major cities around the world. We urge the public to take immediate action to receive the vaccination. There are two phases to the treatment, the first a shot and the second a pill that you have to take within a specific window of time. For the treatment to be effective, it is imperative for you to follow the medication timeline. Your local government, and media will alert you to the next step. Thank you."

Chapter 23

"Hello?" I answer the telephone.

"Come outside now," I am only half shocked at the voice at the other end of the line.

"Come up. I'll buzz you in," I sigh, resigned.

I press the pound key on my phone, which is linked into the building security system. A buzz follows. Moments later there is a knock on the door. I open it to see Adam's angry face. He steps past me without a word. He looks exactly as he did in the garden, though his boyish face had been lined with the years of this life. His brown crop of curls, the curls that I have run my fingers through for millennia, are still as messy as ever. We always incarnated in the same form. We always looked the same

"I saw you on T.V. today," he states flatly. "I flew in as soon as I saw. What do you think you are doing?"

"Sit, Adam, I have a lot to tell you," I explain.

He looks at me warily. This scene seems familiar. I take a deep breath. How can I explain to him that I am giving Lucas a second chance? He will never understand. I am a brave woman, having faced many difficult situations in my lifetimes; however, this is one conversation that I wish that I could avoid.

"Lucas is back," I say.

His face goes blank with shock, "What? How do you know? You've seen him?"

"It turns out that the company that I have been working for was founded by him," I say.

Adam laughs. He laughs so hard that I don't know if he will stop. He has gone into hysterics. "*Lucas founded a company that wants to achieve world peace*? What has he got up his sleeve with that one?" he snorts.

"I believe him," I say, looking into his eyes.

Adam covers his face with his palms and moans, "Eve... not again," he groans in disbelief.

Yes, this is reminding me of the fateful night that I tried to convince him to eat the fruit of Pandora. I don't want to fall into the role of convincing Adam that Lucas is trustworthy again. I won't resort to begging and pleading. I reply shortly, "I've talked to him at length and believe him. He's realized that things have gone too far, and he wants a hand in changing it."

"And you bought it? Eve. No. Don't do this, please?" he pleads.

"I feel like I have to," I explain, trying not to catalogue excuses. In reality, I didn't know why I felt that I had to help; I just knew that I did. How could I explain that to Adam and have him understand? I wished that he would, but I knew that he never could. I just had to stand by my decision, no matter what objections I faced.

Adam sits on my couch. I pour him a glass of wine. He takes it and gulps it down. I sit beside him and we both stare into space, sharing a moment of contemplation. I am sure that he too is transported back to the garden in his mind. I break the silence,

"What are you thinking?"

He looks at me, his face blank, "I was wondering what I can say to convince you to not get involved in this."

"What have you come up with?" I ask.

"I know you. Too well, maybe. I know that nothing I say will convince you of anything once you have made up your mind," he answers flatly. "I could never make you do anything, not for long anyway. *You are a donkey dressed as a mare.* You are stubborn in the subtlest of ways," he pauses. "Can I at least ask why?"

"I don't know why. I just feel that it is something that I must do, a path that I must take. Anyway, if it ends badly, it will just be added to the long list of the things that I regret," I assure him.

An angry blush makes its way up Adam's cheeks. He looks mad. I'm sure that I'm rubbing salt into the wound that I made so long ago. I was choosing Lucas over him, again. I wasn't, of course, but I'm sure that is what he was thinking.

"You are crazy, do you know that? You don't know why you are doing this? Just think, Eve. It doesn't make sense. It's dangerous and I don't understand why you don't see that. The world, your life - it doesn't get any better than this, and no one can help you. Anyone who says that they can, only wants to hurt you. Don't you see? He wants to exploit your hope for his gain. Don't do it, Eve. It never worked before, and it won't work now," his voice shakes with emotion.

"This time it is different, Adam," I assure him.

"Yeah, it's always different, *this time*, but it never is. No one cares anymore. Not about the Earth, not about humanity, not about you - and you shouldn't, either. This is not your battle. It's between God and Lucifer."

"If I can help, I must," I answer, almost mechanically.

"If you do this, I can't support you. I won't help you pick up the pieces again. You will be on your own."

My heart sinks, "I know. I didn't expect you to understand. It's just something that I have to do. That is all that I can say," I shake my head.

"Then we have said everything there is to say," he replies without emotion. He is dead. There is nothing left in him. His outpour of anger was brief and sad. He had given up long ago. He just doesn't have anything left in him. A ghost is a spirit without a body; a zombie is a body without a spirit. That is what he is now, a zombie. That is why we aren't together anymore. I want to save the world; he just wants it to be over.

There is a sense of indifference between us. We both know it. We have reached an impasse as of late. I long to be able to connect with him as we once did, to share the love that we once held, but I can feel that our time together has come to an end. We are just on two different levels. Adam is not wrong, I am not wrong; we have just become so different. He cannot understand why I've worked so hard for redemption. I cannot understand why he could not accept me as I am, flawed though I may be, and love me for my burning desire to be *good*, even if it caused me to make decisions that made sense to no one, not even myself. He saw my efforts as frivolous, as a waste of my time and life.

There was nothing more to say. I had wished there was, many times. I had searched for common ground, but there was none. We had to let each other go our separate ways. We sit in indifferent silence. It's apparent that there is nothing more to be said. Adam stands. Halfheartedly, he hugs me, his embrace as empty as a sieve,

"Keep in touch?" he asks.

"Of course," I reply.

Closing the door behind him, I still feel no emotion. How strange. There really was nothing left between us. We have exhausted our connection. It was not warm, nor cold – it was nonexistent.

Numbly, I go to my room and lay down. I can't sleep. Two hours after midnight I cry my first tear, followed by a river of them. I cry at the indifference, at the lost love. I cry for Adam, and for the nothingness that I feel for him. Everyone has suffered. Me, Adam, Lucas. That is why I must do this. That is why I must take this chance. I cry until I, too, feel nothing and my tears stop as suddenly as they came.

Chapter 24

Global distribution of Pandora has been swift. Enough people have received the placebo shot, and received the Pandora capsule for a critical mass awakening. Three minutes until the time where each of the recipients have been instructed to take the capsule of light.

Tick.

Tock.

Tick.

Lucas and I sit facing each other in the chairs in his office. We brace ourselves for the blow. I began this world with Adam. I may be ending it this very night with Lucas. I couldn't imagine another person I would rather be with in this moment. We don't speak. Our hands are wrapped tightly in each other's. My breath is shallow. Two minutes to go.

"Eve," Lucas speaks.

"Yes?"

"We made the right choice."

"I know."

"I am sorry."

"I know."

"I love you."

"I know," a slight smile pulls the corner of my lips. I squeeze his hand in encouragement.

One minute to go.

He releases one of my hands and brushes his fingers against my cheek, the heat from his flesh trails in an intimate river of love, erasing the memory of every tear that I have shed. The air is so quiet that when an alarm on his watch beeps once, I jump.

"It's time," he says, pulling me to my feet. We walk to the window. The streets a quiet at this hour, especially for New York.

Chapter 25

It took approximately twenty seconds after the global consumption of the Pandora pill for all hell to break loose. There is no order. A full fledge battle amongst the humans, between humans, and the legion of fallen angels has erupted. A global insane asylum. Mothers kill their children, a maternal instinct of protection, then killing themselves. Tortured cries of insanity. Bombs, guns, fires. World-wide war.

The phone rings. I look at the caller ID. It is Adam.

"Hello?" I answer the call.

"Eve. Eve?" Static intersperses the line.

"Yes. I hear you." My heart wretches, "Adam?"

Lucas holds completely still, he is listening to my conversation with Adam closely.

"Eve, I had to call to tell you how sorry I am. I've been horrible toward you for the longest time. I was harboring a grudge. I blamed you. But it doesn't matter. I love you. I am sorry," he speaks with urgency.

"Adam, I love you too."

"I think that this really may be the end. Things are bad."

"Did you take the pill?" I ask.

"No," Adam admits.

"I'm glad." Adam could always be counted on to do the right thing. "Where are you?"

"I am at home, in my basement. What's going on?"

"Everyone that took the pill has had the veils lifted. They can see the spiritual world layered over the physical. They have been woken up to a nightmare, able to see the demonic influence currently holding the world at this lower consciousness level. It is was a shock, even for me. But at least they know, even if they don't know what to do with this knowledge, at least they know their captors."

Adams voice flares with irritation, "This is the cruelest thing that you have ever done."

"It was a hard choice Adam, but one that I had to make."

"It is too much. We will be abolished. The Earth and all of humanity will perish, by our own hand."

"I'm betting that the human spirit rising to the challenge," I say, but I don't sound convinced.

"That is a bet that I would not take. That's not why I'm calling. I called to tell you that I love you. Do you remember Eve, when we were young? Do you remember the evening that you woke up, do you remember what you thought your name was?"

A smile touches my lips, "Yes. Perfect."

"You are. I love you. Even with everything that has come to pass. All of the trouble, all of the trials, every torture we have endured. It was all perfect, because it was with you. I couldn't have asked for a better partner. You are perfect. I wanted you to know. You were the best thing that ever happened in my life," he says.

"Adam, you were my safe space. You loved me more deeply than I could ever comprehend. You are the best part of myself. I thank you for loving me as you have, for comforting me through the years, for letting me be the person that I am, and not trying to control me into what you wanted me to be. You supported me, even when you didn't understand. You are my best friend and the best thing that ever happened to me on this planet. Truly." I had forgotten this love. It had slowly withered over the years, and I thought it was long dead. But in this moment, it rose to greater heights than ever before. "Thank you, Adam. Thank you," I cry.

"You are welcome, my love. I hope this turns out well, but if it doesn't, I will say goodbye, old friend, dearest love. I just wanted to hear you, talk to you, feel you, one last time."

"Goodbye, my Adam. My beginning, and my end."

We both sit quietly. It's difficult to let this moment end, even though we have said goodbye.

"I love you," I weep.

"I love you, too," Adam also cries.

Another moment of silence. It is difficult to let go.

"I will always remember us as kids," I promise.

"Me too. Goodbye, my Eve."

"Goodbye, my love."

Adam hangs up. The line goes quiet. I have said my final goodbye. But there was one more, wasn't there? I look over to Lucas, who is reading a text on his cellular phone.

"Pakistan is gone. They detonated their nuclear weapons. Russia, too."

I sit on the couch in his office mutely.

"Eve. *We knew that global mercy killings were a possibility.* This is too big for most to cope with, even for those in positions of power. Israel may be next."

"How about the U.S.?" I question.

"No word yet."

"Lucas?" I ask a little too calmly.

He moves to sit next to me.

"Lucas, it's time."

"No. We can pull through. *Just give it a little more time,*" he pleads. "Didn't you just say that you believed in the human spirit?"

"Yes, but the planet is being poisoned. There is a simple solution to all of this." I stroke his cheek, "You hold the solution."

"No," he protests.

"Lucas, I love you."

"No," his voice falters.

"Lucas."

He shakes his head. Suddenly near tears, he says, "I can't. I don't know what will become of me, and I don't want to give you up. Can't we stay here, on the Earth a little longer?"

"*He can help.* Change this all back to the way it should have been. *He is the only one.* We can't just let this play out."

"It just seems too soon. I just got you back and now I am going to lose you, again," he cries. "I'm not ready. I need more time."

I stroke the back of his head. It's hard for me to deny him, but I know that this is right. I encourage him, "You must be brave."

"What do you think will become of me?" he asks.

"I don't know," I reply quietly. "But you must go." I stand up, pulling him to his feet, "The time has come."

I pull him into my deepest embrace. Our bodies become one in this embrace. I step on his toes and lean my thighs, abdomen, chest, and shoulders into him, resting my head on his shoulder. This embrace cannot be described. Its meaning is crisscrossed by an eternity of love, devotion, pain, betrayal and redemption, returning to love once again. To say that this embrace was profound would be to understate it. We both know that we are on the edge of real change. Life and death. He pulls back and looks into my face, tears run unnoticed. He looks at me with such love, I feel as if I am looking into a mirror.

"This may be my last moment," he says quietly.

We both cry. He strokes the tears from my face, his fingertips filled with love.

"I'm sorry," he says quietly.

I can see the sincerity in his eyes. The love.

"I know," I cry, accepting more than his apology. For the first time I accept all of him. All of his love, all of his errors, all of his hope, all of his pain.

He dips his head and brushes his lips against mine. In all of the time that I have known him he has never attempted to kiss me, strange as that is; he, the devil had never attempted to cross that line. Now, with what could be his dying breath, he has the courage. Before this moment I would not have accepted his advance, but now, my lips meet his and we share a kiss. In my mind I experience everything - in a stream of images. Every possibility, every moment, every possible reality. We kiss deeply, with love, with tenderness, with tears of sincerity. The kiss lasts for long enough for me to see every moment of three realities flash before my eyes; first, the reality that I experienced in this lifetime, from Lucas' perspective. Second, my life with Lucas had his original intentions of me being his queen played out exactly as he had wished; and last, my life had I never met Lucas at all. *We both see, not just me. And it's too much.*

He pulls away and with tears in his eyes, he says, "It would have been better had you never met me." With a cold resoluteness he turns from me, "I'm ready."

"I love you," My heart speaks through my lips.

He turns toward me, my words softening his self-condemnation. "That is all I ever wanted," he says, completely open to me.

"I know that now." And I did.

Lucas closes his eyes and is transformed. In our last embrace he was restored to the youthful angel he once was, though less glorious.

"Father," he speaks the name he has not uttered in thousands of years.

In an instant the space around us is transformed. We are in the garden again, standing by the lake on the far edge of the orchard, the place where Lucas and I shared our first conversation.

"Brother!" a voice calls from the distance. Jesus and Adam make their way through the brush. Jesus holds his arms out, "Come. He is waiting," he says as he takes each of our hands, leading us through the place that Adam and I had once called home. Adam takes my other hand. I look at him in wordless shock. *How did he get here?*

He smiles and responds to my unvoiced question with one simple promise, "You'll understand soon."

"Adam?" I ask unbelieving, though I know that it is him.

"Yes," he smiles. He looks at peace.

Was it that immediate? Lucas gives up and all is restored? I have so many questions. I look to Lucas who is bowing his head, keeping his gaze astutely on the ground, as if returning a shamed man.

We round the corner, then, we see Him. The One. The Only. The All. Upon seeing the face of the Lord again both Lucas and I sink to our knees and cry. Mine, tears of joy at being reunited with my Father. I am so tired, my journey was so long and treacherous. I am home, restored. The joy at being reunited with Him fills every fiber in my body, mind, and soul. Lucas' tears are different. They are tears of regret. Tears that beg for forgiveness. His sobs moans of lament. Our bodies shake with sobs, throwing off every experience that was not of God, restoring every last fragment until we are whole again. Once our crying ceases, spent yet energized, Lucas and I sit at the Creator's feet looking into his glorious face like schoolchildren. The Creator takes his seat and my hand, offering his other hand to Lucas. A swirl of purple light engulfs our bodies, forming a heart. I close my eyes and allow myself to just sit in the glory that is my original source. My Father, my true home. I take a moment to say goodbye to my old life, my old identity; knowing that after this moment I will never return to the girl I once was. I don't have to suffer being separate from my Father again. I accept him with greater intensity than ever. This is the happiest moment in all of my existences. Every moment, every struggle, every tear is brought back to me at *this* moment. I accept everything. All of the good, the bad and the journey as it was. I am finally home

"You have returned," the Lord says. "Welcome home."

Looking at his glorious face takes some getting used to, for it is far too bright. I can feel every karmic imbalance shifting in every cell of my body. Now, after living all these years on the Earth, where the light of God in all things, even our environment, has dimmed, His light is even more overwhelming than before. It almost hurts, no,

145

not almost, it *does* hurt, but once the pain has burned away every heavy thing in me that is not of my original source, what remains is glorious. I soak in the purity, the powerful single sighted goodness that is the Lord. Lucas, who sits beside me is no longer upright, his torso bends and his forehead rests on the ground. He is again bowing, sharing a very intimate moment as he yields to the Lord.

The Lord brings his hand to rest on the back of Lucas' head. Tenderly, he strokes his hair, filling Lucas with His light, "It has been a long journey, my son."

"It has," Lucas replies as he raises his head to steal a look at the Creator. Immediately his head bows again.

"Lucifer, why do you not gaze into my eyes?"

"Because I am not worthy."

"I grant your wish to look at my face."

Lucas raises his head, like a child. Tears fill his eyes as he looks at his long hated, even longer loved, long awaited Father. This quiet moment is so intimate that I feel that I should look away. I divert my eyes to the face of Creator. He smiles, a tender smile at first, then his smile brightens to one of pure joy. A celestial breeze blows as the wattage of his joy is released through this smile. I have never felt anything like it. Pure joy from the original source.

The Lord turns his attention to me. Again he smiles, "Thank you."

My heart fills with waves of His gratitude. *The Creator was thanking me?* I could hardly comprehend this honor and my body could hardly hold the energy of his words. I was beaming!

"I think that I was following your orders. But I'm not sure. I knew that I had to accept Lucas, but could not explain why, not even to myself."

"Indeed, it was me who was speaking through your heart, for you had worked on the darkness long enough to hear my voice telling you to love the very being that had caused you so much suffering. You are amazing, Eve, and lovely. You have worked through so much. I have seen your struggles and understand more than you can comprehend. You prevailed against impossible circumstances as a warrior for love. I am so proud of you."

His love, the love of the Creator had changed, matured. I understood everything. All of the struggles, all of the tears, the separation. Before, when I felt the love of the Creator it was given,

146

as a gift, one that could not be appreciated to this degree. By betraying him, by taking the fruit, and everything that had come to pass since, many things had happened. One of them being the ability for both the Lord and I to expand our love. He was genuinely proud of me, something that would have never occurred without the darkness. His original love was tender; this expanded love was brilliant, with so much true emotion behind it.

"We have much to talk about, come." The Lord stands. The Father takes the four of us on a tour of the Garden of Eden. Everything was the same. I was filled with nostalgia as we traced my original footsteps on this Earth. Finally, we round back toward the clearing where the forbidden trees lived. As we walk the Lord says, "Jesus. Adam."

Understanding the dismissal, both Adam and Jesus bid us a silent goodbye.

The Lord continues walking, his conversation now with only Lucas and me. "I need to talk with you, privately, as it was the two of you that were the cause of the original fall. I have dealt with Adam already, though he was a bystander in this."

"How did he get here?" I ask, running the possibilities through my mind.

"Just as you did. I brought him here." The Lord smiles, knowing that he is being coy. "He made a great sacrifice in staying with you, proving that he was noble and true. He is a hero and has been rewarded as such."

I remember the last time I saw Adam, he did not look like a hero to me. He had given up. He seemed a ghost, a zombie, apathetic and sad.

The Lord laughs, reading my thoughts, *"Eve, have you learned nothing?"* He chastises affectionately. "A true hero does not return home from battle in a pressed uniform, hair perfectly coiffed, riding his noble steed, flags a-blazing. The truth is not a fairytale; it is hard, dangerous and many do not make it. If you do – the reality is that you *just* made it, having lost a lot, having seen too much, having been damaged seemingly beyond repair." He smiles, the remembrance of some unseen memory brings an expression of pride to his face, his eyes well with perfect tears that glimmer like crystals in the sun. "And it is my honor to repair that which has been lost, stolen, and exhausted. *I am the Victory Parade.*"

147

And then I see it. I see Adam through the Lord's eyes. He *is* beautiful in all of his battle wounds. His failings are not a dishonor; they are beautiful, because they were earned in a world that pushes you beyond your limits, and kills your soul. We did not live in Paradise, we lived in Hell. His wounds were earned as stripes are by a general. *I am sorry that I judged him so harshly. I am sorry that, once again, I judged him by outer appearances and did not look with the eyes of my heart.* I have not changed, even after all of these lifetimes, I am still judgmental and unfair. *I was so busy condemning Adam for what he was not that I did not see what he is.* What's worse is that this was a revelation from the Lord, not a conclusion that I had come to on my own, and that pained me even more. *What is wrong with me?* The Lord answered my thoughts,

"And those, are *your* battle scars." He stroked the back of my hand with his thumb. He tapped my chest with the lightest pressure three times and the sorrow inside of me falls away. "Just as Adam promised, you will understand everything soon. I have been waiting for this moment for a long time. It has been lonely for me, not to be with you. Loving you from afar. I am glad that you are home," He spoke to us both.

I look up in surprise, *"You were lonely?"* I ask, shocked. It never occurred to me that He would suffer. I couldn't see beyond my own anguish. Sometimes my suffering was so great that I could not bear to live, much less look outside myself and consider His. I imagined Him living in heaven without a care in the world.

"Paradise is not a home without you. You are my children. I have been watching you, waiting for you." The Lord stops abruptly before we come to the tree line of the clearing. He looks at Lucas and I, a thoughtful look crosses his face, "We are to come to the trees where you made the original choice to be separate from me. I'm sure that you have learned a lot from the repercussions of that decision. There is one more choice to be made. Come," the Lord motions for us to cross the tree line.

As Lucas and I step over the threshold of the clearing we see something that confounds us both. We look at each other with questioning eyes. Our bodies lie sleeping under the withered Tree of the Knowledge of Good and Evil. Adam's lioness stands guard, pacing the space between where we stand and our resting bodies. I did not understand. There, beneath the tree, was my naked body -

148

lying peacefully in slumber, my skin as plump and as new as the day I was created. Lucas lies next to me in his green flowing robes, as glorious as the day that I first met him. There is a youthful innocence to these bodies, one we both had lost long ago. It was like seeing myself as a child.

Tears move me, and I lament every moment that I had faced that has withered my spirit from this original splendor. I was perfect.

Lucas cries, too. The Creator passes us, walking to our sleeping bodies. He crouches down and examines our supple forms, "Come." He kneels.

Following his orders, the lioness stands down as Lucas and I approach. I sit next to my body looking at my beautiful sleeping face. Lucas does the same, looking in wonderment at all he once was.

"There is a choice to be made. One of you will die today. It is not yet determined which of you will cease to exist. Your bodies that lie here are the bodies that you inhabited just before you tasted the light of Pandora. I would not allow my perfect creations to be tainted with the hard life that would follow tasting the fruit. When you tasted the light, in the moments that you blacked out, I forged a new body for you. Ones that would be resilient enough to endure the darkness to come. Your innocent nature, your original spirit still inhabits this form lying here. You are bound to this body, spiritually.

"I have protected and kept these bodies safe from harm. Any goodness still in you is felt and experienced through this body. When you meditate or pray, you open the connection to this body and taste paradise, if only for a moment, to replenish your soul. The times in your life when you experienced love and contentment for no reason, those where the times where the spiritual channel was free from the clutter of your mind and you were able to feel your connection to paradise."

I am overwhelmed by this realization. I cry as I stroke the velvet cheek of my original body. I am so beautiful, so pure. I look over to Lucas who is shaking with sobs. His head rests on the chest of his former body. I remember his monstrous appearance when he came to me and I understand this strong emotion. He had fallen so far from his original state. I had withered and hardened, but even in my darkest hours I was still resembled my original form.

"One of you *will* die today. If you would like to say your goodbyes or if there is anything that you would like to say to your pure self, I offer you that opportunity now," the Lord offers.

This is it. The end of my long journey. Live or die, this is the end. Tears run down my face. I realize the preciousness of my life. I am overwhelmed with a sense of nostalgia, treasuring every moment that I've lived: the joyful moments, the sad ones; the moments that were so difficult to get through that I cursed the day I was born. In *this* moment, all of those moments carry an unspeakable value, not because they made the experience of my life good or bad, but simply because they *were the moments of my life*. I look lovingly upon my pure face, this face that I may never see again, this body that I may never feel again,

"Hi, Beautiful." A smile touches my lips. "I've missed you. It's been so long. I'm sorry that I left. I've been through a lot," I laugh nervously. "I'm sorry I didn't stay and that I wasn't here to use you to your fullest potential. You had to sleep through your entire life. You didn't get to see, or feel, or touch, the true beauty of life for yourself. It wasn't fair, to either of us. If I had the chance again, I would be better. I'm sorry that I did not appreciate you when I had you." I held the hand of my pure self and stroked her fingertips. Leaning over, I kiss my own lips with such sincerity that my original form smiled softly in her sleep.

Lucas, to my right has his own conversation with his body. He was speaking through his sobs in a language I did not understand. The language of the angels, his original tongue. What I could understand was the emotion behind the words he uttered. It was truly heartbreaking; yet somehow the deep recesses of my heart were touched by such nostalgic mourning. He was magnificent in his newly-restored humility. Gratitude and regret wrapped beautifully around each note that he spoke. Liquid diamonds glimmered down his cheeks. As his emotion calmed, he began to sing a soft lullaby to his former self, a lullaby filled with such love that my heart opened and was pierced by the energy of his words. He smiled softly and stroked his face and hair as he would a child's.

The Lord himself was moved, his face contorted into the purest expression of grief for the slightest moment, then it passed. Through tear-filled eyes, he spoke, "Which of you would like to say goodbye?"

"The choice is ours?" I ask.

"It always was," the Lord answered.

I immediately spoke, "Me. I will."

"No, Eve." Lucas looks shocked, "Don't. I will, Lord."

"Lucas, please. Let me. You have suffered enough. Live, for me."

"Eve, I will not let you sacrifice yourself for me. It was my fault, all of it. The only way to redeem myself would be for me to allow you to *live*, as you would have, had I not interfered."

"But you just opened your heart again," I protest. "You have come so far, and it would all have been for nothing. Don't give up now. I have lived enough. I am done, Lucas. Let me, please."

"No, Eve. You don't mean that. I have been restored. That is enough for me."

"No. Lucas."

"I love you, Eve."

"I love you too," I cry because I know that I am the one who will live.

Lucas looks to the Creator, "I choose this."

The Creator nods. "By choosing this, you allow Eve to live."

Lucas looks at me and nods once, "It's what is right." Though his words were brief they were laden with a thousand *I love yous*. My heart swells with the unspoken goodbye.

"Lucifer, please retrieve a piece of fruit from the Tree of Life," God says.

"Can I say one thing to you, Lord?" Lucas asks, earnestly.

"Yes," He concedes.

Lucas' voice shakes with an overwhelming emotion. "Thank you for creating me. I'm sorry that I became prideful. I'm sorry for the trouble that I caused. You were my first love. I always loved you, somewhere inside, even when I hated you. I don't understand why I… You did not deserve any of the strife that I caused. I ruined everything. Not just for me, but for everyone." Tears run down his cheeks now, "Thank you for the chance to live. I'm sorry that I did not accept that gift. I don't know what was wrong with me, but I see now that I was wrong. You are God. *My God.*" Lucas bows. A loud sob escapes his lips and he breaks down completely. His tears are brief, but intense. God allows him to release all of the unexpressed emotion; he patiently strokes Lucas' hair until his mourning ebbs.

When Lucas stands I can see that he has finally found the peace that he had been searching for. He walks to the Tree of Life, reaching his hand high above his head. As he plucks the fruit, the fruit of Life, his entire body goes aflame with a gold celestial light. He shines brilliantly, even more brilliantly than he had in my visions of him in heaven. Holiness has been conferred upon him once again. Through his sacrifice, his nobility has returned. He can die a hero. I can't imagine a world where he doesn't exist. He was such an important part of history. I have loved him, hated him, cursed him, and now, I bless him. I wish that there were another way. I wish that I could save him.

Returning, he kneels between our sleeping bodies. He holds the molten fruit above my lips.

"The heart, Lucifer," the Lord instructs.

Lucas moves his hands above my resting heart. He looks at my face: a face aged with the lines of many lifetimes and says his final word to me, "You taught me how to love again."

Oh, God no. I realized that this was it, and we didn't have enough time. I wish that I would have let us linger on the Earth just a little longer, as Lucas had begged. In my haste to get back to God I had sacrificed Lucas' life. A price he was willing to pay, for me. I hadn't realized that I would lose him. I hadn't even thought about it. I didn't want to. I was so focused on my re-entry into Paradise that I hadn't considered anything else. I will never see him again after this moment. I had so much to say, but not enough time. I realized so much in these last few moments, and I will never get a chance to tell him. *It wasn't his fault.* The realization struck like lightning. *It wasn't his fault. He didn't trick me. I chose. I chose to eat the fruit.* I had spent an eternity avoiding this realization, keeping my mind wrapped in blame because I was afraid to accept responsibility for my actions. I didn't want to feel the pain of my own karma because I was afraid, somewhere deep inside, afraid to be *wrong,* afraid of what that would mean about me. So instead, I blamed *him*, assigning myself the role of victim. And that also was a choice. I saw it so clearly now, and I *wanted* to accept responsibility, it burned within me.

"Lucas! No." I look to God. *"Please. Don't let him do this."*

Until this moment I had no idea how much he meant to me. I really did love him, every part of him, even the part that had aided me in betraying the Creator. I have forgiven him. It wasn't even a question anymore. Before this moment I have never known *complete* forgiveness, I have always held something back, reserved the right to recall the error, to not trust, but now, it's gone. I love him. It wasn't his fault. It doesn't matter. I just love *him*.

"*Lucas, don't,*" I plead, sobbing. "*No…* " I turn to God, "There must be another way, please?"

The Creator puts his hand on Lucas' wrist, compelling him to stop. His expression changes, He is thoughtful,

"There is a way," the Creator says. "But it will involve a sacrifice on both parts. Neither of you will be restored until this sacrifice is completed. You will have to go back."

Go back to Earth? It was the battleground that claimed every ounce of goodness within me and tore my soul to shreds. It was a never-ending hell that I'd barely survived. I look around Eden – it seemed to shimmer, more glorious than I had remembered. Once again, I had a choice to make. *Was I willing to sacrifice paradise so that Lucas could live?*

Chapter 26

"Yes. We'll do it," I speak quickly, before this momentary bravery evaporated into thin air.

Hope flashes in Lucas' eyes, "Eve?"

"We'll do it," I say again.

"Eve, no." Lucas touches my hand, "You can't."

"*We* can." I brush his cheek softly.

"I can't take paradise away from you. Not again," he protests.

I look around Eden. Of course, there was a part of me that wanted to stay – it was my home. But my heart couldn't imagine a world where Lucas didn't exist. What good would paradise be if I was mourning the loss of my oldest friend? What pleasure could I take if he was gone? *Forever?*

"This place isn't so great," I laugh.

"Eve," Lucas speaks my name severely.

I turn to God, "I have made my choice."

"Lucifer, are you willing to return?" the Creator asks.

Lucas looks into my eyes, searching to find the reason that I would knowingly give up paradise for him, especially after all that I had endured. I nod my head in gentle encouragement,

"This is real," I whisper softly.

The expression on his face is one that I shall never forget - it was pure gratitude. He had been forgiven, offered a second chance, and he knew, beyond a shadow of a doubt, that he was loved.

"I will do everything in my power to prove to you that I am worthy," he promises.

"Very well," the Lord concedes. "You shall have what you have asked for. Upon your return to the Earth your mission is simple: you must provide the antidote to the ills of humanity."

"The nectar from the Tree of Life?" I ask, conjuring a plan for global mass distribution, just as we had with Pandora.

The Lord laughs, "It is forgiveness. Jesus went as a messenger for this, but the people weren't ready. Now that Lucifer has tasted true forgiveness – what better person to share its message?"

"You want us to become Christian Missionaries?" Lucas asks. A slight smile passes his lips, catching the irony.

"Not exactly. I want you to instruct them on how to forgive and be forgiven. You can only teach what you have experienced for yourself. Your message will be powerful because you rebuilt your spirit with such sincerity. You did the impossible, Lucifer. You - the devil, found the angel within you again. And it was through love. That the essence of what you will share. It isn't a religion, or a belief system. It's just your story."

"That sounds almost too simple," Lucas says.

God laughs, "Every mission seems simple when received in paradise. Figuring out how to do it on Earth, without being thrown into a mental institution is the difficult part. Also, holding onto your mission when times get tough can seem almost impossible. But there is power in sincerity. And you have a miraculous story to tell."

"How will we know when we have succeeded?" I ask.

"You will know," the Lord smiles. "Once the planet hosts a peaceful society for three consecutive years, I will restore it to a modern paradise, for everyone."

"Three years of peace?" I think about the current condition on the Earth. "That will take a miracle."

"You have performed greater miracles than this. It may have been a long journey, but you never gave up. You brought Lucifer back from the depths of hell. Your love is the miracle, Eve."

"When do we go back?" Lucas asks, bowing his head.

"Now," the Creator answers.

"Now?" I gulp. It seemed too soon.

"There is no time like the present, or so they say," the Lord says. "When you return, you will not be able to cross dimensions, Lucifer. Just those who have come before you, you will be bound to a human body."

Lucas looks up, "Will I remember?"

"No." The Lord looks to me, "but she will."

The Lord presses Lucas' wrist, compelling him to insert the fruit from the Tree of Life that he still holds into my resting body.

"The heart, Lucifer," He says softly.

Lucas looks at the surging miniature sun in his hands, positioned above the chest of my original body. I kneel beside him, placing my hands over his.

He turns to me and mouths *I love you* silently as we submerge the light from the Tree of Life into my chest together. I lightly rub

155

the back of his hand with my thumb, a small gesture to say my goodbye. He won't remember me after this moment.

My original body inhales, pulling the life deeper inside. Swirls of golden colored life energy surround both Lucas and I -as we kneel beside my original form. My vision goes dark and I cannot see anymore, yet I feel my body falling forward - as if I had fallen into the void. I sense that Lucas there with me. In nothingness, we float. My consciousness observes a thousand black scorpions turn into doves that take flight. My awareness then spins through seven vortexes of light: red, orange, yellow, green, blue, purple and white.

Chapter 27
The Beginning

The first breath is always the best. How that sweet breath was breathed into me, filling my lungs, traveling like a cool fire throughout my entire body. Then I felt a pulse, surging through me. As I breathe, I feel my awareness expanding to my face, brightening in relaxed waves of light. A circular expansive energy travels through the back of my head, down my spine, legs, feet; up my shins, abdomen, chest, feathering through the planes of my face once more in soft waves of life. I didn't breathe this breath; it was breathed into me.

I stretch my body. The deeper I stretch, the more intense the pleasure, the movement activating the muscles in my feet and legs. It all feels breathtakingly good, like my body is supposed to move this way. With a moan of pleasure I stretch my arms. I hear birds chirping their lovely song, the faint sound of a car horn in the distance. I open my eyes, turning my head to identify the sound. I recognize where I lay. I am under a tree in Central Park. A pain in my abdomen catches my attention.

I look down and see my uncovered breasts, skin aglow with the health of paradise. I am naked. My social instinct tells me that this isn't appropriate in this time and place, so I devise a plan to find clothing without being noticed.

I turn my head, peering across the expanse of grass in search of Lucas. But I am alone. I feel another sharp pain in my stomach. It takes my breath away. I clasp my abdomen and discover that I am nine months pregnant. My water breaks, and I realize that I'm going into labor. I am certain that a son will be born to me on this day. I will name him Lucas. And he will be loved.

Epilogue
Rebirth

"Mama?" Lucas blinks his large green eyes eagerly. He was a darling five-year old boy, with pale, smooth skin that still possessed a whisper of the incandescence from our days in the garden. His short crop of black waves glistened in the light, as soft as the moon's reflection on a night time pool.

"Yes, Darling? I smile at my precious child and understand why, once upon a time, he was the most beloved of God's angels.

"Where did babies used to come from?" he asks, looking expectant. There was a calmness about him, an unwavering soft glow of light. His eyes observed everything, quietly considering all that he encountered. He was purity untouched by desire, intelligence untainted by knowledge, spirit untamed by mind. He looked to me for everything; how the world worked, where to orient himself toward it, what to hope for and what to believe. I was his mother, the source of his information, the benefactor of his love, and the single most important relationship in this human life.

"Where do you think they came from?" I ask, closing the refrigerator door and kneeling to his level. I'd carefully phrased the question to understand what type of answer he expected. This boy of mine, who doesn't remember his dark past, will one day inquire about his origin. Of this I am sure. Knowing how to tell him, discerning the exact moment that he is ready to shoulder the heaviest burden known to any man, that, I was less sure about.

"I think they came from heaven," he states definitively. "But Angelisa says they came from sex."

"You are both right," I say.

His expression is calculating as he considers my response, "Mommy?"

"Yes?"

"Did *you* have sex?"

An unexpected burst of laughter spills from my lips. He was a delightful child. "You were different," I explain, sidestepping the question. "You came into mommy's tummy directly from heaven." I shower kisses on him and we both fall to the ground, where I continue to pinch the muscles around his ribs with gentle repetition, which sends him into a fit of giggles and wild involuntary body movements. "Because you are an angel!" I tease, crawling over his body on all fours and biting his neck like a puppy at play. But the reality was, I wasn't teasing.

Laying on his back, breathless, he pauses, reaching to caress my cheek with his baby velvet fingers, "Are you an angel too?"

"Not like you." *In every jest there was a kernel of truth.*

"Mommy?"

"Yes?"

His brow furrows, "What is sex?"

"Oh boy," I exhale, sitting back on my heels. "What do you think sex is?"

He raises his little body into a sitting position. "When a girl and boy kiss… *on the lips*," he answers, grimacing.

"It's a little more complicated than that," I explain. "When two people are first deciding if they like each other - they may hold hands, just to see if it feels right. After they hold hands, they may kiss. And if they still like each other after that - they may decide to French kiss," I explain, my voice taking on the tone of a kindergarten teacher.

"Is it called that because you do it in France?" he asks, furrowing his brow. He was very serious.

"That's a good question. We should google it," I suggest, reaching for my smart phone on the kitchen counter. I type Lucas' question into my favorite on-line encyclopedia and read the contents of the page aloud, amending the entry to a level that a kindergartener could understand, "They call it a French kiss because at one time the French were known for being the most romantic people on the Earth. So, no matter where you do it, it's still called a French kiss."

"But why do they call it a French kiss and not just a regular kiss?"

"Because it's a special kind of kiss, reserved for people who want to know each other in a special kind of way. It's like a regular kiss on the lips, but both people open their mouths and touch tongues."

"*Eww… Gross…*" Lucas grabs his throat and falls back to the ground as if he were just poisoned.

"You won't always think so," I assure him, pulling him upright once more. "It's a natural way to get to know each other on a chemical level. Plus, most people think it feels good."

"What does it feel like?" He squints, as if bracing himself against a heavy wind.

"Do you remember that time you licked the nine volt battery?" I ask.

"It made my tongue feel funny." He sticks his tongue out, face contorting with sensory recall.

"That's exactly what it feels like," I smile. "It feels kinda funny at first, but after you get used to it, it feels kinda nice."

"And you do it with a... *a girl?*" Disgust twists his features. He was all boy; snips and snails and puppy dog tails.

"You can do it with anyone that you love in the special kind of way that I was talking about. Someone that you want to be romantic with," I reaffirm. "When you want to be more than friends."

"And that's how they used to make babies?" he asks.

"There is a different kind of kiss that used to make a baby. When a man and woman kissed with their bodies, not their mouths. That is called sex."

"But sex doesn't make babies anymore?"

"No sweetheart, it doesn't."

"Why not?" His eyes narrow as his young mind tries to figure the puzzle that had alit the people of the world with despair.

It was a mystery that I didn't have an answer for. The only thing that I knew was that the moment that my water broke, when Lucas and I had returned from Eden, the hospitals were overrun with pregnant women going into labor. By the time that he was born every pregnant woman on the planet had either delivered, or miscarried, depending on the time of term. There were no more children born on the planet after Lucas, he had been the last. That was five years ago.

"They don't know. But all of the best scientists are trying to figure it out," I assure him.

"But we can still have sex?" he asks thoughtfully.

"Yes," I confirm. "It's still a way that you can become really close with someone that you love."

"I don't ever want to have sex."

"Then, you don't have to, but someday, you may want to. And if you do, I want you to know that it's natural, and perfectly okay."

He doesn't answer, he just shakes his head side to side emphatically, eyes wide with a concern that borders on terror.

"Well then, that's okay. I'll just keep you forever and ever." I pick him up and hug him tightly. Of course, I don't want to stifle his development, but there is a part of me that doesn't want him to grow up either. I wish he could stay my little Lucas forever, because of the difficulties in life that I know he will face.

"I will mommy," he promises, hugging me tightly. "I will stay with you forever."

I let myself rest in the embrace of my little boy, willing the moment to last. But one thing can always be counted upon, *tide and time wait for no man.*